ZARA

ZARA

JOYCE STRANGER

THE VIKING PRESS / *New York*

Published in 1970 by The Viking Press, Inc.
625 Madison Avenue, New York, N.Y. 10022

SBN 670-79633-6

Library of Congress catalog card number: 70-104131

Printed in U.S.A. by Vail-Ballou Press, Inc.

This book is dedicated to Gwen Best,

with my love, and to her husband Mac Best,

who so loved horses and inspired me with

his memories of them—and, sadly, died

before the book was finished.

This book is fiction. All places in it and all people in it are imaginary and not based on any living person. The horses do not exist.

ACKNOWLEDGEMENT

I would like to thank numerous people connected with the racing world who have helped me acquire information and the brain specialist who provided the solution to one of my problems, and Geoff, who patiently answered a great many medical questions. Also Mr. R. F. Whitney, who answered my questions about racing, and the numerous authors who helped me understand the problems of training and management.

ZARA

The mare was gleaming gold and dynamic movement and sliding, shining muscles. She was flowing mane and flying tail, racing against the wind. She was vividly aware of warm sun above, and cool grass beneath her hooves; of the background murmur of running water; of birdcall, an angry shouting at a questing dog-stoat sleeking through the shivering stems. She was conscious of an intense joy in living, of power, and of pride that arched her slender neck. Her wide wise eyes observed the world around her, saw the sky above her, and her constantly flickering, sensitive ears moved as a sudden gust groaned among the branches.

The man watching her wanted her more than he had ever wanted anything in the world. He was driven by a physical need, a wild desire for possession. He wanted the feel of her warm hide against his hands, the thrill of watching her endlessly galloping over springy turf. He wanted to caress her slim neck, to speak to her and have her conscious of him, turning her head so that her dark eyes could look at him with affection. In time he would breed from her, mate her to Midnight, the splendid black stallion that was lord of his stud, and in time her foal would run beside her, delicate, incredible, a minute creature of utter beauty.

His mouth was dry with excitement. There never had been such a mare. She was bred from the desert wind and the moonlit night and the shimmering stars, bred from the raging need of man to find perfection. And she was perfect. Nothing flawed her. He craved her as a woman covets a brilliant gem, as a child hungers for the glowing moon.

The man beside him watched him with amusement. They were leaning on the broad white rail that edged the paddock. Beyond them the field sloped to the bank of the river Weere, a shallow rock-bedded trout stream that gave its name to Weeredale. Beyond the stream the rock-ribbed ground sheered to a long hill crested by trees. A sparrow-hawk hovered, watching the blown grass.

Jed Howarth savoured the sunshine and the view and the running mare as he savoured life. The Manakee stud was his dedication, but the beasts in it were more to him than money. He, like his companion, had been born to live with horses, had ridden from the day he could walk, had thought and talked horse talk in every waking moment of his life.

Jed was a huge man, and looked even bigger in breeches and shining boots and sheepskin jacket. His dark hair, aglint with copper flecks, was short-cropped; his face, brown from days in sun and wind, was deep-jowled, hinting fat. Brown eyes watched the world from under black stiff-haired brows. His big red-lipped fleshy mouth was often quirked to laughter.

He laughed now as the mare bounded past them, hooves drumming. He knew horses, having bred them, sold them, and bought them all his life, and she was the best he'd ever handled. He corrected the thought. She was the best he'd ever seen. He turned to speak to his companion, and changed his mind. Richard Proud was spellbound, unable to take his eyes from her. Nothing else existed in the world.

Beside Howarth, Proud was dapper; slender and dark-haired, his chin already, at three in the afternoon, needing a shave, in spite of the utmost care that morning. Eyes grey and so deepset under long dark lashes that they seemed black, brooded in a face that was harsh and angular, but that softened as he watched the mare.

She threw up her head in a gesture of intense pleasure and called to the brilliant sun. Richard Proud clucked to her as she trotted towards them, and she came to him, treading delicately on deceptively fragile hooves, and dropped her muzzle to his palm, breathing warmly, and huffed to him.

He was lost.

Jed Howarth relaxed. He knew he had made a sale, but he was in no hurry. He was a patient man who could wait his time, and he was as clever at handling people as he was horses. The mare would go to an excellent home. The Proud stud, though small, had a splendid reputation, and Richard Proud could turn the utmost villain into a well-mannered beast. The mare was no villain. She was perfection in shape, in temperament, and a miracle of speed.

Jed watched the mare. He did not want to sell her. She was beautiful. But he could not afford her. Feed and keep cost more each year, and there was much competition among breeders. More people turning to the horse for relaxation also saw its possibilities as a source of income and produced foals, oblivious of the true cost and also, only too often, unaware of the rules of good horse management, so that many animals suffered from their owners' unthinking ignorance.

Richard was watching the mare as she moved, noting the lines of her, the elegance, and the strength. She had never foaled. She was four years old, and ready for the stallion, but Jed refused to breed a young animal, maintaining that there was too much wastage. Horses were not fully grown till four, and too many of them, foaling when young, or raced too often when young, ended up ruined for life, unable to last more than a couple of years at their peak. After that, all kinds of weaknesses developed. He was a perfectionist, and so was Richard Proud. And it did not pay. That was the plain hard truth of the matter, and the reason for so many young horses having to show their paces, or for the young mares to produce a foal too soon.

Sometimes a horse brought a big price. But not often. Meanwhile there was the stud to maintain, buildings to repair, fences to keep in good order, and money flowing like water for food and hay and bedding, and for wages for the men. And on top of it all taxation, which was crippling.

Richard Proud was thinking about money too. At times he envied Jed, who had a much bigger establishment, and could afford good grooms. At his own stud he kept ten mares, and the stallion Midnight, and a young stallion that he used as a teaser, to see if the mares were ready to accept service. If they were not, he ran the risk of having his best stallion kicked or bitten, and that was disastrous. He ought not to buy another mare, but this one looked as if her progeny would fetch higher prices than the foals he bred from the mares he already owned. And he needed money. She was an investment, not an extravagance. Her breeding was superb, her ancestors all winners.

He needed funds for the upkeep of the stud, and for the Manor Farm attached to the little manor house that ate up even more cash. And money to keep his wife happy. If that were possible.

He thought of Stella for a moment and frowned. There was no end to her extravagances. To the parties that she gave. To the outrageous clothes that she bought, flashing from town to town in search of new fashions in the MG that he had given her, after she had badgered him almost to breaking point, and that she sent hurtling down the lanes as if the devil himself were chasing her.

She had asked for an expensive emerald ring for her birthday and accused him of neglecting her when he at first refused. He had sold a colt to pay for it, a colt that he had trained, that had gone on to win races for its new owner and changed hands for five times the price he had received for it. It would have paid him handsomely to keep the animal.

Now she wanted an Aston Martin, and seemed unable to understand the basic facts of life on a stud farm, expecting him to sell three mares to buy it, or the bull that was the pride of the Manor Farm. She could not see that the mares held the future and that the foals they would bear would bring in the money she craved. Or that the bull produced fine daughters. That came of being captivated by a pretty face, he thought regretfully. He had gone overboard for conformation and not for character. It didn't work—not with women. And the character she revealed over the last year belied her beauty. There seemed to be very little sense in his wife's elegant head.

Abruptly, the worry that he kept hidden flared to angry life. Stella had changed . . . was changing. When he married her she had been gay and lighthearted and had found life fun. Now . . . no one who knew her in the old days would recognize her. He did not know what was wrong, why she was so restless, so irritable, so demanding. And he could not reach her. They had forgotten how to talk to one another, somewhere, in the years between.

She was still beautiful. And, on her good days, as gentle as she had been when he first knew her, so that he found himself hoping that life would resume its former peaceful track, and that she would share her time with him, and with Sue.

Then, quite suddenly and unpredictably, she changed and was another woman, alien, thoughtless, and unkind. He did not want to think about her. He looked towards the meadow.

The mare was rolling in the grass, her legs kicking towards the sun. She was vibrant with life and excitement, unable to contain her energy, running for the thrill of spurning the ground beneath her flying hooves, her head turning when the men spoke, listening to the timbre of their voices, like the pleasant soothing deep sounds that always reassured her when any of the grooms were near. Jed chose his men carefully.

Richard wondered what they called her. He cast a reluctant look over his shoulder as he turned away. She was speeding towards the rock-bedded steam, where terraced limestone was worn smooth by the thrust of rippling water, now shallow in its bed, but when the sky poured rain, swelling to a peaty torrent that foamed thick and brown and ferocious over the channelled rocks, threatening danger from the floods that often ravaged in the Dale.

Soon her groom would come for her and rub her down. Richard envied him. He wanted to handle her, to savour the thrill of owning her, to watch the shining coat shine even more as he worked on her, to sleek the

8

silken mane and tail. In her stall at night she would
wait patiently for another sunny day and the feel of
cool green grass under her hooves and the bliss of rolling under the wide blue arch of the sky, hearing new
sounds and smelling new scents and rejoicing in utter
freedom.

A donkey shared her field. He had been lying beneath
a tree, and now trotted towards her. Honey-coloured,
shaggy-haired, with gentle eyes and coal-black diminu-
tive hooves. He was very young and he rubbed affec-
tionately against the mare, and she huffed at him and
then raced him to the water, where both heads dipped
to drink.

Richard Proud drew a deep breath.

"She might be barren. It's a risk," he said.

Jed grinned.

"It's a risk with all mares. Never can tell till you've
tried. Nor with the foals. But her mother threw good
foals, and her sire gets winners. So she stands an even
chance of doing you proud."

Richard winced at the pun. Just like Jed.

The fields lay serene in the sun, trees bulking large,
where the horses could shelter. Weeredale was wooded,
its sides sloping gently, not rising stark and bleak towards a barren skyline. Trees bordered the stream, giving shade in hot weather.

Overhead the clouds gathered, heralding night. The
dipping sun streaked them with scarlet and black, and
the water in a pool at the edge of the Weere caught the
colours and tossed them back to the sky. Rooks flew overhead, cawing loudly, their wings darkening the branches
as they settled to roost. A wood-dove crooned nearby.
The mare listened to the sounds, her ears showing interest, her eyes turning to pick out the rooks, to discover
the wood-dove. She watched the men as they left her,

moving uphill towards the stables, opening and closing
the gate and fastening the horse-proof latch that she had
tested several times, in the hope of freeing herself and
galloping gaily to discover the outside world.

Richard glanced around him as they walked back to
the house. Over forty mares grazed in the paddocks.
The foals ran races, vying against one another. They
were now weaned and separated from the mares. Many
of them would be sold in the yearling sales next spring.
One small creature, intensely curious, came to the gate
to stare at the men, and then, when Jed spoke to him,
lost his nerve and cantered back to the others, hiding
himself among them, sheltering from the unknown
world.

Beyond the paddocks were the long neat lines of
loose boxes; the barns, filled with straw for bedding,
and hay for feeding; the storehouse, and the harness
room; the room where the men ate, and the bunk-
house beyond it. Next door was the foaling block with two
white-washed stables, one on either side of the supervi-
sor's room, where a man could spend the night and keep
an eye on two mares at once through spyholes in the
doors. It was more luxurious than many hospitals, and
as clinically sterile. The telephone communicated directly with the vet.

Proud noted everything with a connoisseur's eye. The
yards were swept clean, and hosed. The fences trim and
freshly painted that year, the gardens neat and well
kept, although now, in late October, there was little left
but a thin blooming of roses and a freckling of dahlias.
The trees were turning colour, and some already welcomed winter with branches to which only a few last
yellow leaves clung tenaciously.

The house was large, an uncompromising block of
solid dressed Yorkshire stone, built to withstand the

frequent gales and the wintry bleakness that clothed the Dales with snow. It sheltered under the hill, looking out over the stables and beyond to a wide sweep of country where high stone walls marked the boundary lane, and along the curve of the opposite slope to the old road that travelled the heights and lost itself in trees. Sheep roamed, cropping the scanty grass, their white bodies the only sign of movement on the other side of the Weere.

Although the house, outside, was stark and uncompromising, the inside was warm and welcoming. In the study a log fire blazed comfortingly, taking the chill from the autumn air. Richard Proud accepted his host's whisky and spread himself in one of the brown-velvet-cushioned, leather-upholstered armchairs that gaped invitingly, his feet stretched on the shaggy black hearth-rug among the three cats and five dogs that sprawled at ease in front of the blaze.

A Labrador opened one eye and closed it again, a brown mongrel came to greet him with eager flailing tail, the two beagles thumped companionably, and a wire-haired terrier licked Jed's hand and then rolled onto her back, legs wide open, chin extended, to be rubbed with a booted foot, while one of the cats, stretching a paw, accidentally clawed the smooth bare belly and the bitch sat up, startled. She went to Jed for consolation and he petted her, fondling her soft ears, while she looked up at him with adoration in her brown eyes.

Richard sighed.

Stella hated cats, could not bear them coming near her or fawning round her legs, and she would not have a dog in the house.

She had changed so much since he married her. Then she had vowed she loved animals—especially horses. They had owned a black cat and Richard had had his own black Labrador, Scot. Over the years she had altered completely. Or was the change recent? He could not decide. Her ways distressed him and her manner hurt him bitterly. She had furnished their home with ideas gleaned from glossy women's magazines, attempted to follow the latest smart decorator or to copy one of her rich friends, liking to be in vogue. The result was bleak as a shop window, a soulless showroom that neither he nor Sue dared spoil and that Stella wished were better furnished, hankering always for materials and antiques that he could never afford. In the past year her taste had become more and more bizarre, her purchases extraordinary, defying understanding.

The house was not a home where a man could stretch at ease, and kick a log fire to an ardent blaze, and sit with a retriever's head against his shoe and a cat perched on the back of a chair, books and papers tossed negligently on the floor. Jed's room was lived in. His books were piled in an untidy heap, the ashtrays were meant for use and not to add a note of colour to the room, the chairs were shabby and comfortable and relaxing. No one would grumble at untidiness, or hurry to set the cushions at a neat angle as soon as a chair was vacated. No one had straightened the rumpled rug or placed each chair in precise symmetry. He sighed deeply, wishing this were his home. Stella was becoming more unreasonable every day.

Sue would love this room. He grinned ruefully. She had been on holiday in France with the school that Easter, and Stella had had her bedroom redecorated as a "surprise." Not even he had seen the final result, and he had been busy in the stables when Sue came home

and, after one look, rushed downstairs.

"Come and see," she said. "Just come and look."

He had gone and stared in disbelief at his wife's idea of the perfect teen-ager's room, where pop singers' posters and an astonishing mural of whirling colours glared from the orange and black walls, chairs as hard as tree trunks stood in mathematical precision, the bed had been changed for a divan covered in zebra stripes and massed with enormous cushions of lime and emerald and jade and purple.

"She just has to be crazy," Sue had said, in utter horror. Richard, for one terrifying moment, wondered if the statement were true, and then dismissed it. Trust her mother not to know that she hated pop music, had conventional tastes in pictures, and that no girl could ever relax in such a screaming maelstrom of colour. No wonder the child spent all her time in Vence's shabby cottage, where his plump Yorkshire-born wife, Sarah, was always surrounded by a permanent aura of baking bread and new-made cakes, and the cottage was a home.

"How is Sue?" Jed asked, as if reading Richard's thoughts.

Richard shrugged.

"Lonely, poor kid," he said, surprising himself as he spoke. It was something that he had only just recognized. He was lonely himself, but he was always busy. Sue helped him when she could, but few of her friends lived near, and next summer she was to take her O levels. Examination work kept her well occupied.

"Haven't seen her for a long time," Jed said.

"She's working for exams. This damned educational system . . ."

He left the sentence unfinished.

Jed nodded.

"The kids are in the rat-race from the day they start school. Geoff was home this weekend. He takes his finals this year. Wants to go on and do a Ph.D. He looks as if he's been holed up for weeks with his books. I sent him out with his sister to get some fresh air up on the moors. Di's working for her A levels. Damned if I think it's worth it, at times. All work and no play . . ." Jed was not bookish himself. His children surprised him. "I suppose they get it from their mother," he added.

Richard nodded. Jenny Howarth loved reading, and was usually to be found curled up in one of the big chairs, a book in front of her, lost to the world. Her family teased her about it, and she smiled at them, and opened another book.

"Where is Jenny?" Richard asked.

"Gone shopping. She's going to breed donkeys. Trust Jenny to try her hand at something she knows nothing about. And I bet she'll make a go of it. She's fallen for the little fellow down there with the mare."

"Sue would love him," Richard said.

"Just as well. I think you'll have to have both of them if you have the mare. She won't settle at night unless he's brought in with her. And they both fret and refuse to eat if they're apart."

"Worse than people," Richard commented. He looked at the firelight reflected small in the glass of the bookcase near the fire. It was filled with shabby-covered well-read books. Jenny's glasses were on the table beside it, her knitting thrown carelessly down on a stool, three stitches off the needles where a cat had pulled at the tempting dangling thread. Her cardigan was on the back of another chair, brief reminder that she was not far way, that she would soon return and fill the room with her presence and her quietness. The flame flickered and died, symbolic, he suddenly thought, of the warmth he had once felt for Stella. He was aware of

sharp bitterness. He did not want to leave. Here a man
could relax, could sprawl at ease in the armchairs,
among the friendly huddle of dogs and cats, and savour
living.

"I'll have to go soon," he said reluctantly. The
whisky was drained almost to the last dreg, and he refused another, as it was a goodish drive home. One of
the cats had left the rug and jumped to his knee, where
it slept, curled up, its soft purr throbbing. He stroked
the shining tabby fur and the cat stretched its head,
eyes shut, asking for its throat to be rubbed. The throbbing grew louder.

"You're damned lucky, Jed," Richard said and imme-
diately regretted the words. He was a reserved man,
hating to reveal anything of himself or of his own disen-
chantment with his life. If it were not for Sue, and the
horses . . . He looked bleakly into a future in which
Sue was grown and gone away, or married, and he had
only the stud and the farm left. It was a lonely vision.

"Fifteen hundred guineas, and cheap at the price,"
Jed said, not wishing to pursue that subject. He had his
own opinion of Richard's wife, and it was not flatter-
ing.

They had agreed on the price while standing in the
field, looking over the mare and chaffering like two
tinkers at a country fair.

Richard walked over to the window. He could see the
far paddock where the stream sparkled under the last
dying light. The mare was standing motionless, regal in
her perfection, looking towards the house. She turned,
and he wished that he could paint or find words to express the utter impossible beauty of her, the fineness of
line, the slim legs, the dancing hooves that trod on air.
A groom was coming to fetch her, and she walked towards him, the donkey following. It was a good sign.

She knew men and trusted them, and would be biddable. The man put on her head rope and she followed quietly, her honey-coloured companion as close as her shadow.

There would be no new car for Stella. She would not be pleased. She had been trying to persuade him to pay a deposit so that she could drive over to see her sister next week and show off her latest acquisition. Mary's husband was very wealthy, and Stella always wanted to compete.

He was tired of trying to appease her in her attempt to keep up with the Fosters, and Joe Foster neither noticed nor cared about the rivalry between his wife and his sister-in-law. Possessions were not important to him. Richard liked him, and the two men were friends. Joe would appreciate the mare. He had an eye for a horse, although he did not ride himself.

"Fifteen hundred guineas," Richard agreed.

The mare was finer than any mare he had ever seen. She would be the darling of the stud, petted by the men and boys, cared for by her owner, coveted by everyone who saw her. He would have to make sure that she was not spoilt. And her foals might be worth a fortune.

Sue would adore her.

He did not know her name. He hoped that she had a name that suited her, a name that spoke of desert winds and moonlight and starlight, a name that told of her beauty.

Again Jed anticipated the question.

"Her name's Zara," he said. "I've got a copy of her breeding somewhere. I'll let you have it. One of her grandfathers is a son of Hyperion."

Hyperion. A name to conjure with. No wonder she was elegant. And there was more than a chance that her

foals would be winners. Two big sums when they
changed hands and he could expand the stud, build
new stables, take on more men, keep more mares. It
was a daydream that he longed to make reality, and at
times he regretted having to keep his feet on earth. If
he dared speculate, or take a risk or two, or even gamble . . .

But he was not a gambler. Not as a rule. Perhaps—
for once, he was gambling on the mare.

He went out into the yard where his Morris station
wagon waited beside Jed's lean Jaguar. He saluted Jed,
and took a last look at Zara as he drove away. She was
walking to her stable, gentle as Vence's old dog. Zara. It
conjured visions of doe-eyed girls in harems, of Eastern
lands where the best horses were bred, visions of the
Godolphin Barb, of the Byerley Turk, of the Darley
Arabian. Shades of the most wonderful horses in the
world. Richard, like his daughter, was a romantic, lov-
ing music and poetry, and often oblivious of the more
mundane aspects of life. It was pleasant to dream. Tomorrow the mare would be his. Tomorrow she would
be part of his stud, standing quietly in his stables,
learning to know her new master. Tomorrow.

He was four miles beyond the turning to his own
home before he realized that he had overshot the corner
and driven straight on. He reversed, and, driving back,
his exultation was mingled with guilt. He could not afford another mare.

The yard was deserted when he drove in. The house
waited for him; smaller than Jed's, but also built of
Yorkshire stone. As he walked up the steps into the
hall, depression drifted about him, cloaking him.
Laughter and voices and a babel of music came from
the big drawing room. Damn it. He'd forgotten that
Stella was giving a party. He glanced at his watch. It

ZARA was later than he had realized, and past eight o'clock. He was hungry but no food would be ready. Stella would have been busy all day with preparations for her guests. He had no desire to face the crowded room, or join in the laughter and inane chatter and drinking.

He turned and ran down the steps, away from the house. He crossed the yard and hurried into the little lane. Opposite the gate cottage windows were lighted, spilling welcome onto the muddy rutted surface. The front door was ajar.

Richard pushed it open and at once was enveloped in warmth. The two dogs lying on the flagged uneven floor thumped their tails at him; Pru, the Siamese, came to him and made love to his ankles, purring and rubbing against him, ecstatic at the contact. Sarah Vence, plump and red-cheeked, her hair in a loose untidy bun, her white apron spotless, was ladling broth into a bowl.

"There's some for you too, Mr. Dick, if you want," she said. The accent was there, faint and unmistakable, friendly and welcoming, telling of her upbringing in Wharfedale, not so very far away.

Sue sat at the end of the table, her school uniform out of place on her elegant little body. Although she was dark and as plain as her father, she had her mother's slender grace and beautiful walk.

"So you've escaped too, Dad?" she said, and they were conspirators, grinning at one another. His eyes savoured her.

He did not kiss her, knowing that she hated any kind of demonstration, yet sometimes he longed to hug her to him as he had when she was tiny and came running to him for comfort when she was hurt. Stella had no time these days for the child, and made constant comments about her plainness.

"School okay?" he asked, not knowing what to say.
She nodded.

"Sit down and drink oop. It's good soup," Sarah Vence said, and Richard laughed, knowing he need not praise it for her. He drank and watched her bustling about, broad as she was high, homely, reliable, and capable, friendliness emanating from her. Everything she touched turned to comfort, from the plumped cushion in an armchair to the pillows in the bed if anyone was ill. It was a good job Sarah was there, he thought, as she buttered scones and cut cake, chatting to Sue. No one else would have looked after the child when she was poorly, or listened to her when she was well, even. He was no good at woman talk.

The smell of new-baked bread and hot scones and currant buns made his mouth water, and he piled his plate and stirred the strong tea, and listened to the cuckoo in the clock call the half hour and the budgerigar in the cage in the corner sing out in sudden competition.

"You can eat your supper here," Sarah said. "There'll be nobbut nibbles over at t' house, alawand." Sarah never spared her criticism. "Leave t' cake till after." She took from the oven a steaming pasty that begged to be cut. She sliced it in four, and divided it onto four plates and added peas and potatoes, taking care not to mar the clean red cloth. Vence, opening the door, sniffed his appreciation, and blinked and grinned at them.

Jim Vence was a small man, half the size of his wife, his brown face wrinkled and creased and merry, his tongue always ready to tell the truth and shame the devil. Sarah believed in outspokenness and honesty but saw no call to be as blunt as a sow's whisker, and often chided Jim for lack of tact.

Richard had known Vence all his life. He had been

stud groom when Richard was still at school, had helped him out of scrapes and spoken up for him to his father, who had been a harsh man, demanding impossibly high standards from his only son. A bitter man, left a widower when the boy was born, his life made among the horses, with little time for Richard, who would have lacked all roots if it had not been for Jim and Sarah, who came as his nurse and stayed on when she married Jim.

Sarah fed him and bolstered him when he was miserable. Vence showed him a world that his father did not share, casting a fly over the trout streams in the dusk when the fish were rising; walking the moors, watching a sparrow-hawk hover and kill; knowing where the hares ran and the rabbits bred and setting snares to catch them. Not even Sarah knew of these exploits.

Helping on the Manor Farm in lambing time; creeping out of bed at night, out onto the cold moor, where the sheep bleated and waited their time; knowing the sudden excitement of a second life where before there had been only one. Watching over a mare, and seeing her foal take its first breath, its first suck, its first step; learning about horses by working with the boys in the frosty mornings. Now Vence managed the stud farm. And taught Sue some of the things he had taught her father, but not, Richard hoped, all of them, recalling exploits on the moors with a falcon that took pheasants and the illegal trout that they cooked over a stick fire, down on the rocks by the stream.

Vence, eating his pasty, was conscious only of a feeling of intense satisfaction. He had been all over the stud that afternoon, chided a stable boy for forgetting water for one of the horses, found one of the beasts slightly lame and treated her, and studied the mares and foals. Of the ten mares nine had foals, and one of

those had twins. Only one barren among them and
they'd sell her in the next beast sale, for a child's riding. She was gentle enough and Sue often rode her.
Might have known she wouldn't do well, that one.
Funny breeding in her line, and just as well to stop it.
Ten foals for the home stud from Midnight and then
the twenty he'd got for owners who had sent their
mares to him. They had all gone home now. Been too
busy to breathe in the early part of the year.

Could do with another mare. A real winner, a
beauty, Vence thought, and then drank a sip of tea and,
remembering, almost choked.

"Phone call for you," he said when he had recovered.
"From Mr. Hanbull, at Regency School. Says to go
over. Something he wants you to do for him."

CHAPTER *two*

Roy Hanbull was Headmaster of Regency School, a vast greystone block situated on the other side of Weeredale, almost six miles away. Richard was glad of distraction. The sound of music and laughter was louder; he did not want to join Stella and her friends nor did he wish to encounter his wife later, when she was fey with too much wine and he was sober. He never drank overmuch, not caring for the feeling of irresponsibility that came after several refills, and always concerned to be ready to deal with any emergency on either the Home Farm, or the stud farm. Fate had no time for those who lost control.

He enjoyed driving at night, and after he left the school he could take the long road home. Stella would have gone to bed. He did not want to talk to her. Wine lent her eloquence, and she would ask again for an Aston Martin, or for money to paint the house tangerine or to buy another fur coat. If he agreed, she would remember and keep him to his promise, and if he disagreed she would make a scene that would disturb him and upset Sue.

Raucous laughter echoed from the house as he backed the estate car out of the garage and turned towards the lane. Vence opened the gate for him, and then he was away, the house and the party a memory, the engine note steady and sweet, the car moving effortlessly over the road. It was good to drive. Nearly as rewarding as handling a horse, man and beast working in unison, centaur-like, almost fused, interpreting one another's thoughts.

Night had hidden the ribbed slopes and the wooded tops. Moonlight glinted on greystone walls. An owl flew alongside the car and then swooped away, whooing. The headlights flung strange leaping shadows across the road, so that it was easy to believe that there were uncanny creatures abroad in the dark, elongated trolls that raced towards him, brandishing weapons, and dropped away again; tiny dwarfs that grimaced from the hedgerows. Richard was glad of the stick that he always carried in the car beside him. He liked it there when he was bringing home the men's wages from the Bank. These days, one never knew. . . .

Mist hovered above the road as he climbed the hillside. The moon picked out the water, far below, and the mist curled and filled the valley. Mist hung between the high stone walls that soon enclosed him on either side, hiding the fields. And then the walls vanished and he was on the moors and the headlights reached into nothing and the road stretched, tunnel-like, in front of him, bordered by darkness, and he was relieved when the climb ended and the labouring engine took the car round the wickedly steep hairpin bend, and over the crest down towards the school. He drove through the sleepy village where greystone houses huddled together, piled one above the other, shape merging into shape in the darkness beyond the street lamps; past the church where Mousy Thompson had carved the pews, each one autographed with a tiny harvest mouse that the children loved to look for on a Sunday when the sermon was dull. The church itself had a squat stone tower and was low-roofed, and yews grew thick and hid the tumbled gravestones.

The leaves had not yet left the rhododendrons that flanked the winding gravelled drive to the school. The great house, where once a branch family of Cravens had lived, was bright, with lights in every room, the windows bare and blank and curtainless. Boys' heads were outlined, bent over their evening work. A gowned master stood on the steps, his robe lifting in the breeze as he savoured fresh air and a welcome cigarette. He nodded to Richard, who was well known at the school. The older boys were borrowed to help on the farm at haytime, during the week-ends, and rewarded by rides on the horses. Richard kept two hunters and Sue's grey, as well as three colts that he was schooling and that Sue hoped to jump at near-by shows the summer after next. Muffin, the grey, was willing but loved speed and did not jump well. There were also, often, a couple of racehorses in training.

The headmaster's flat was part of the east wing of the building. Walking down the desolate corridors, his feet echoing on linoleum, Richard only half saw the portraits of former headmasters and patrons of the school that hung on the walls. Old-fashioned, dark, and undistinguished, their gilt frames were heavy and ornate, and the boys had names for all of them. The Growler and Old Nutface. Nobbly Conk and Scrawny. No one remembered their real names or what they had done to earn a place in the school's reluctant memory.

Heavy oak doors closed the classrooms. A boy ran down the corridor, ducked under Richard's arm, and ran up the uncarpeted stairs, his feet thundering. A
master shouted.

"Hey, that boy there. Walk, don't run."

"Boys!" he said morosely as Richard passed him, and turned away, a heavy-set man with a tired face and resigned expression. Years of teaching the same things, of telling the boys to behave, of fighting to instil some sense into them, had worn away his freshness. Richard thought of the stud and the stallion and of the mare that was to be his in the morning, and was suddenly elated, knowing that his life with all its imperfections was better than this prison in which boys were moulded to be like other boys, to be good citizens and conform to the rules that society imposed on them.

Some would break away, wander the world, would never settle, would seek the truth that lay beyond the stars and be branded as outlaws. The rest would jog along until they lay in narrow graves, and would never know what life could have offered them.

Roy Hanbull was thankful to relax in his own flat where none of the boys ever came. He had a sitting room next to his study in the main block, and here he entertained parents at tea, and also entertained sixth formers who were soon to leave, and tried to discover their hopes and plans, their aims and ambitions, and to guide them into a career that would suit them.

He was a small man, stockily built and swarthy-skinned, dark-eyed, with an intense enthusiasm that brought from his staff miracles of loyalty and also touched to life some of the latent qualities in the boys who responded to his dynamism.

He was always engrossed in a new idea, a new excitement, and at the moment his Lower Sixth were busy rehearsing a puppet play that he had written, so that they could tour the wards of the local hospitals at Christmas time. Boys needed occupation. They needed to be useful. They needed responsibility, and he saw to it that his school practised what he preached. A half-finished puppet lay on the table, ready to be dressed by his wife, and he was scoring out lines in the script that he had written, adapting the words, making the sentences easier to learn and to remember, and adding phrases that would bring the play to life. He had listened all the afternoon and knew where the scenes fell flat.

Pegeen, the gigantic Great Dane, stretched herself and came to meet Richard. She was quietly demonstrative, and she put both huge paws on his shoulders and licked his face. He laughed and pushed her down, and she sighed deeply. No one ever seemed to appreciate her greeting. Richard sensed her disappointment and stroked her head, and she leaned against him adoringly.

His news was too good to keep. It was spilling from him.

"I bought a new mare today,' he said. His mind was full of her, of her beauty, her superb lines, her future as the mother of the best foal in his stud, in the county, in the country. He saw the foal in imagination, pacing delicately, a glorious creamy gold, enormous eyes watching the world. He saw it later, running at race meetings, faster and fleeter than any horse yet bred, a legend in its lifetime, a horse to join the past heroes, walking at the head of the Shades of Arkle and Golden Miller, Jerry M and Manifesto, Cottage Rake and Easter Hero. Crowds would cheer it as it sped to victory.

"A good one?"

"A beauty. She's costing me fifteen hundred guineas," Richard said.

"I thought that Stella wanted an Aston Martin? And that you were pushed for money?" Roy looked at his friend thoughtfully. Old Dick was haggard and tired, and the lines of strain in his face seemed to deepen

daily.

"Stella can go without for once," Richard answered shortly.

He swung the stick that he had taken from his car. He looked down at it, frowning. It was a strange stick, hand-carved, and very old. The head of a tiny ugly man leered wickedly from the crest of hickory wood, and round the thick stem a snake twined, its own head protruding below that of the man. Sue hated it, saying it was unlucky, but it had belonged to his grandfather and, so the old man said, to his grandfather's grandfather.

Holding it, he was reminded again of the white-haired, white-bearded old man, bedridden after a fall in the hunting field, impatient, angry, cursing at those who came near him, hurling anything that came to his hand at the fools who were tardy in answering the thud thud thud of the stick on the floor, bellowing with rage at the doctor who could not help him to walk again.

Vence had sometimes pushed him round the stud in a wheel chair, and the old man had thundered his wrath at grooms and stable boys, had yelled at the least sign of untidiness and disorder, and then, left by himself at his own request in a corner of the stable, talked to the mares in so gentle a voice that it was hard to believe he was the same man.

"T'owd devil," the lads had called him, and rightly. He would have approved of the mare.

Richard put the stick on the floor, and Pegeen mouthed it and then, unexpectedly, backed away, growling.

"That's odd." He put the stick on the top of the grand piano.

"Sue says it's unlucky. Pegeen seems to think so too."

"She's daft, is Pegeen," Roy said. "Dick. Why don't you divorce Stella? Or . . ." he hesitated, suddenly careful.

Richard walked to the window. It was dark outside and he could see nothing but the reflection of the big room, where chintz-covered armchairs contrasted with the cherry-red carpet that was shabby with long wear. He could see a picture on the wall mirrored before him, a Dutch interior that he had always admired. Nobody but Roy and the Vences called him Dick any more. Nobody but Roy would have dared ask such a question.

"I can't," he said at last. "God knows I've reason. But I can't drag it all out in court, because of Sue. It wouldn't be fair to Sue. Perhaps when she's older . . ."

He hesitated.

"Besides—she used not to be like this. She's always been headstrong and extravagant—that's her mother's fault. She used, when she was alive, to keep comparing me with Joe Foster. But Stella used to be fun—I keep hoping—these changes—there must be some reason—"

"Is it fair to you?" Roy asked.

"Life's not fair," Richard said harshly. "There's nothing I can do, not yet. But if ever she tries to teach Sue her ways . . . then I will."

"She won't." Roy Hanbull was positive. "Sue's all yours, and she couldn't live like her mother."

The clock struck ten. Each tiny chime tinkled in the quiet room, and the Great Dane lifted her head, her eyes watching the silent men. She nudged her master's foot, and he fondled her ears, but with his eyes on Richard and only half his mind on the bitch, so that she pawed him anxiously, trying to attract attention to herself. He rubbed her head and she leaned against him and yawned.

Richard roused himself and came back to the fire. He held his hands to the warmth of the blazing logs, although it was not cold. There was so little warmth in
his life.

Hanbull turned his head as one of the school maids entered with a tray.

He poured coffee and handed Richard a cup, and then took his own and also took three pieces of Turkish delight from a small bowl on the table.

"You'll get fat," Richard said. "You're as bad as you were at school."

He sat down.

"Vence said you wanted me."

"Yes." Roy Hanbull was suddenly ill at ease, and Richard looked at him, astonished.

"It's Chris," Roy said at last. He moved his hand suddenly and Pegeen yelped. He had caught her ear between his hand and the hard edge of the chair. He stroked her, instantly remorseful.

"I thought he was better," Richard said.

"He is, physically," Roy answered. He seemed unwilling to come to the point of the conversation. "Considering he was paralysed for nearly six months, it's a miracle that he can walk at all. As it is, he only needs a stick and a support on his right leg, and the doctor says that those muscles will strengthen too and no one will guess that he ever had polio. Only . . . Chris won't give it time. . . ."

Richard Proud nodded.

Chris had always been headstrong, from the time he learned to walk and found that his elders would never allow him to explore where he wanted: along the bank of the river, in the old quarry, among the farm machinery. Animals fascinated him, but he had not enough patience to learn to handle them, so that he was always in trouble. A bite from a dog that he had approached too turbulently, a kick from a strange horse that he tried to ride bareback, a fall from the top of a haystack on which he climbed when he was very young, trying to grab one of the farm cats. He was even more reckless when he grew up. He climbed the rocks at Castle Naze, alone on the high bleak scars where all the winds of hell met and tore at those who dared the escarpment, and fell fifteen feet, and broke his ankle.

He had fallen off his bicycle, racing another boy, and broken his arm; fallen off a horse, jumping too high a fence, and broken his collar bone; skidded on his Honda and sprained his wrist. And then he had developed polio, caught from one of the boys at school, and lain, angry and resentful, able only to move his eyes, hating the world that had taken him and treated him so brutally.

Movement came back, and he punished his body, driving it to work for him, persistently torturing muscles that screamed in protest, giving himself no rest or respite, and, now that he had to wait for time to heal the last disability, turning in savage fury on anyone who tried to help him, or suggested methods that might make the return to strength easier, or asked him what he wanted to do or where he wished to go.

"There's no living with the boy, and Janet is only staying sane on tranquillizers," Roy said unhappily. "He's no time for any of us, and he won't take advice, or help, or come anywhere with us. He's atrociously rude, and now, this last week, instead of continuing with his exercises and swimming, he's relapsed into apathy. He just sits. . . . The doctor says we must make him take an interest in things, but that's all very well. I don't know how. I can cope with any boy in the school, and I'm beaten by my own son," he ended bitterly.

"What do you want me to do? Talk to him?" Richard asked.

Roy hesitated.

"More than that. The doctor says that riding might help to do the trick and to strengthen those leg muscles. He always wanted to be a jockey. Remember?"

Richard did remember, and remembered too the drama on the day that Chris first realized that he had grown much too tall and too heavy ever to race. Fate never did seem to compromise with Chris. He had railed furiously, and tried to starve to get his weight down and only desisted when he developed polio.

"If he could live with the Vences for a while . . . to give Janet a break. She's had as much as she can stand . . . and I've had nearly enough. If there's a horse he could ride . . . and he could give a hand round the stables. . . . He might be easier with you, and better away from home. And he and Sue get on well. It would be company for Sue. . . ."

"How old is he now?" Richard had never thought to hear Roy plead for anything.

"Seventeen. Eighteen next month."

"If the Vences agree. It depends on Sarah. I'll ask her tonight and let you know. If she says it's okay send him over as soon as you like. If he'll come. Have you asked him?"

"I'll jump that hurdle when I come to it," Roy said. "If he won't he'll have to go somewhere else. Apart from anything else he's causing trouble in the school. If anyone looks at his lame leg, he attacks him. Lashes out with his stick. He simply goes beserk. Fortunately they're learning not even to glance at him and the masters have taken to keeping within sight when he's out with the others."

He sighed again.

"Have some Turkish delight."

Richard took a piece absent-mindedly.

"You eat to console yourself and I buy myself horses I can't afford and shouldn't buy," he said.

"Not only eat. There's always the school," Roy answered. "I can bury myself in work. Janet can help Matron, but she can't get away from the boy as I can. Children. You build your hopes on them, dream about them, plan for them, and then they kick you in the teeth."

"You two look as if you're indulging in some kind of intrigue," Janet Hanbull said, coming into the room and walking over to the fire. She was blonde and delicate, slightly built and smaller than her husband, and her vivacious face looked unusually tired.

"Chris has gone to bed."

She dropped on to the settee beside Richard and poured herself a cup of coffee, refilling the two other cups.

"I'm whacked," she said.

"He's coming to stay with us for a bit," Richard said, not intending to make a promise but anxious to ease the worry on her face. He had always been fond of Janet.

She looked up at him, and then suddenly swallowed and turned her head away to hide the tears that forced themselves from her eyes. She had no resilience, these days. Pegeen walked over to her and sat with her head on her mistress's lap, and consoled her by licking her hand.

"I've bought a new mare." Richard was anxious to change the subject, to distract her, to give her time to control herself again. Janet was normally so self-possessed. "A beauty. You must come and see her. Her name's Zara."

"What colour is she?" Janet sipped her coffee and managed to smile at her husband. Reassured, he took another piece of Turkish delight, and she moved the bowl out of his reach.

"You'll turn into a pig," she said.

"That's what I told him. The mare's gold. The colour of sunlight. You never saw anything like her."

Richard remembered her, standing in the field, her coat burnished by sunshine, moving superbly, bending her head to drink. "Such a mare," he said softly.

"What did you name the foal that I saw last week?" Janet asked. "The one you intend keeping as a stallion."

"Vence named him," Richard said and grinned as Roy and Janet laughed.

"Minnow? Or Tadpole? Or Sturgeon?" Janet asked.

"No. This one isn't too bad. It's Brama, for the bream, which at least is better than Trout and Salmon. When you look in the stud book and find Proud Trout and Proud Salmon . . ." Richard laughed again. Vence was a passionate fisherman, fishing in every moment of his spare time, and left to himself all the stud would have fish names. Luckily he allowed Sue to name half the foals, so that as well as Proud Blenny there was Proud Shadow and Proud Silver and Proud Firefly. And Sue had named Midnight, who was blacker than the Weere Pot, where pot holers were often marooned when it flooded after rain. Richard had been down there once, but never again. It seemed to him the mouth of hell.

"He's called his sow Minnow," Richard added, and they all laughed. "She's the biggest Middlewhite sow you ever saw," he went on. "And she's expecting. So she's vast."

"I must come and see her," Janet said.

Richard stretched and took his stick from the piano.

"I hate that ugly thing. Why don't you get rid of it?" Janet asked, and Pegeen, seeing the rounded base near her nose, growled again and moved away.

"Sue hates it too. But it's a family heirloom. It can't be that unlucky. We aren't an unlucky family," Richard said.

"That depends on what you call luck." Janet looked at the stick and made a face. "Your grandfather broke his back. Your mother died when you were born. Your father was killed by a flying bomb. Give it away, Richard."

"I've often wondered what it's supposed to represent," Roy said. He looked at it curiously. "That looks like an African voodoo head."

"It was made in Yorkshire," Richard answered. "There used to be a plaque on it, with the maker's name, but one of the dogs chewed it off. Lots of people have wondered about it. One man says he thinks it represents the Tree of Knowledge with the snake curled round it, and perhaps that's Evil looking out of the tree. The old man in the antique shop in Huddlewyke says it's the Laidly worm that devastated Yorkshire in the old days and devoured maidens and burned villages."

"That legend came down from the time of the Viking ships," Roy said. "With their dragon prows and their men raping and burning and pillaging. No wonder a lot of Yorkshire was devastated. And in those days when the Dales were all forest it wouldn't be easy for a man to move far or to find the truth of a tale."

"I still think it's unlucky," Janet said.

"I can't give bad luck away, any more than good," Richard answered. He looked at the stick, and the tiny head seemed to leer back at him. He shivered. "I used to think when I was small that if grandfather struck the ground hard enough the deadly plagues of Egypt might come forth, or the snake twist away from the stick and grow to a huge size and say, 'Master, what is thy will?' like the genie in the Arabian Nights. If I could do it now—" He struck it suddenly on the floor and Janet jumped and cried out "Don't."

"I'd wish for money to buy ten more mares," Richard
said.

The door opened.

"Oh—you're still here," Chris said rudely. He had flung a dressing gown over his shoulders and his dark hair was on end, giving him the appearance of a badly ruffled kestrel. "I thought you'd have gone by now."

Roy's mouth tightened, Janet's expression changed to anxiety, and Richard tapped the stick on the carpet.

"The Luck of the Prouds. Or is it the Luck of the Devil?" Chris eyed the stick for a moment. "Mother, I can't sleep. I want one of your sleeping pills. Where've you hidden them?" His voice was rising. Roy's expression was thunderous, and Janet looked anxiously from her husband to her son.

"I'll ring you later." Richard went out into the night, unescorted, made uneasy by the tension that filled the room behind him and wondering what Vence would say when he told him Chris was coming to stay for a while.

He drove back through the darkness, which was made blacker by clouds that shrouded the moon. The mist had cleared. A little wind keened in the wires along the roadside, and in all the night nothing moved. He was a fool, he told himself, watching the road ahead, lit by his own headlights. As if he hadn't enough trouble of his own, without adding Chris to them. Some people never learned.

He rounded a bend too fast, and the stick slid sideways and fell off the seat with a clatter that made him jump.

A fox ran into the road and he braked. The wheels locked and skidded. He eased the brakes, the car corrected itself, and the fox vanished into the night.

"It can't be unlucky," he said. He had never been superstitious. But in that brief moment uneasiness possessed him, and he almost threw the stick out of the window into the ditch. Another car passed him, headlights briefly dazzling, and, reassured, he left the stick where it was, marvelling at his own gullibility.

It was later than he thought. Vence's cottage was dark, and only the hall lights shone, waiting for him, in his own house. Sue always made certain that they were on if he was late.

He garaged the car, thankful that the party had ended. Sometimes Stella's festivities continued far into the night. He lifted the stick from the floor and looked at it. The tiny evil head wore a sardonic grin. Suppose it were unlucky? Suppose that there were devils and angels, and that his rational world, based on things that were tangible, was also peopled by unseen forces?

It was very late and he was tired and over-fanciful. He put the stick back on the passenger seat of the car. It was useful, and it was absurd to believe in luck, either good or bad, although Sarah, he knew, was sure that the old woman at the end of the village was a direct descendant of witches and had the evil eye. If a cow developed mastitis or a horse went lame, Sarah worried lest they had offended old Maggie, and even he, seeing the bent old woman in her long black skirts, a shawl round her shoulders, untidy grey hair escaping from a man's cap and her toothless mouth forever a-mumble, felt uneasy when she was near.

He unlocked the stables. He could never go to bed without a last look at the horses, anxious to see that all was well. There were five mares in each block, and the weaned foals were in a third block. He looked at the rounded quarters filling each stall. Heads turned towards him, and he patted each one, speaking gently.

Midnight, across the far side of the yard, in his own

stable, heard his master and called. One of the mares answered.

"Hush," he said, stroking her neck. "Or we'll all be in trouble."

Stella was a light sleeper, and he did not want to face her tonight. Time enough in the morning. He sighed, and turned out the light, and locked the stable door, and shot the bolt. The mares in the other block were quiet. He went to talk to Midnight, who hated to be ignored and was kicking the wooden door, his shod hoof thunderous.

The stallion was unpredictable. He rarely misbehaved with either Richard or Vence, but he disliked two of the stable boys, who were both afraid to go near him, as he tried to bite, or to kick. Richard suspected that they were not horse-wise, and that either their voices or their abruptness of movement annoyed the big black beast. He was almost seventeen hands, and his progeny were all brilliant . . . not one failure from Midnight. Richard gave the stallion a carrot and stroked his neck. It was the only time that he ever gave a titbit, last thing at night, before he went to bed.

"Quiet now," Richard said. A shadow moved behind him, and he turned his head to see one of the stable cats slip across the straw. He went over to the empty packing case that they had left in the far corner. Sure enough, four small blind kits lay inside. Kitlins, Sarah always called them. The little cat jumped in and curled among them, and opened her mouth in silent threat. Richard smiled at her.

"Good puss," he said. She relaxed, but continued to watch suspiciously until he was gone.

The house loomed black against a starlit sky. The trees moved behind it, guarding it against winter-wild winds. In the hushed yard, Richard was conscious of the breathing of the horses, a giant sigh, almost in unison. The farm cattle were dark beneath the trees. Soon he would move the mares to the far pasture and bring the cattle to graze the rough grass that they had left. An owl plaint sounded, low and mournful. Sad as the souls of the dead in the churchyard at the end of the village. Yet the outside world was friendlier than the house that waited, and he sighed again as he went inside and climbed the stairs to the black and white room that his wife had furnished for him. It always seemed sacrilege to discard his clothes in such pristine tidiness.

He would have to tell Stella that there was no question of an Aston Martin. He was not selling any more colts. He was going to school them and Sue was going to jump them if they showed promise. And he was going to race them. He had a trainer's licence, as he had always wanted to train as well as breed. It was some years since he had raced one of his horses. It was time he considered himself. Life was chasing by and there were so many things to do. He had never bred a superb foal. He would like to build up the stud until it was as large as in his grandfather's heyday. It was easy to plan at night, midnight thoughts that in the cold light of day would seem absurd.

As he drifted off to sleep he wondered if he would be able to keep his resolution, and he dreamed uneasy dreams in which Jed delivered the mare, but when he went to take her from the horse-box she had vanished and his wife sat inside instead in a vast chintz armchair and mocked him with her laughter.

CHAPTER *three*

Jack Braithwaite, manager of the Manor Farm, was jubilant. He had bought a new ram.

He had been up since four-thirty, overlooking the two men as they milked. His foreman, who was ill, complaining of a touch of flu, had telephoned the night before to say he was feeling maffly. Old Adam clung to his dialect words.

"Can't trust nobody these days," he'd said. "Better get out and watch t'lads at milking. Need watching, both on' em. All slape and promise when they're warking."

Nothing had been slipshod or badly done that morning, Jack thought with satisfaction. The cows were in the covered yard, waiting for daylight. He wanted to move them on to new pasture. The old one was a fair mess. Poached to a morass by the gate. Too wet by half, this back end. But he wasn't moving cattle in the dark, not down the lane and across the road at the bottom. Fellows came a sight too fast round the corner, and there'd be an accident before long. But not to his cattle.

He went to gloat over his new acquisition. He had been to the Swaledale ram sales at Kirkby Stephen the week before, and his purchase had arrived last night. A huge beast, with curling horns and an arrogant head on him, glaring angrily now, not liking his new quarters at all. He had cost over £400, and even that was not a high price. Another breeder had paid £1400 for his beast, and a fine beauty he had been too.

But there was nothing wrong with this fellow.

Richard, up unusually early, already unbearably excited, although the mare was not due till late morning, saw the light in the yard and came across to Jack.

"Nice beast," he said approvingly.

"Got him for four hundred and twenty. I didn't go to the limit."

Richard nodded. Their limit had been six hundred. There were three hundred ewes on the hills. His land included the adjacent rough land, where the hill sheep could graze profitably, but nothing else found much nourishment. He wanted to improve his flock, and the Swaledale would do that for him.

Vence joined them and looked thoughtfully down at the ram.

"Bass'ld be a fine name for 'im," he said unexpectedly, and Jack and Richard laughed.

"He's named already. Pedigree long as your nose, but his calling name's Bramble. Seems he was born in a bramble bush, plumb in the centre, and they had a merry time getting him out. Nobody knows how t' ewe got through wi'out getting tangled."

"I've got a new mare coming, Jim," Richard said, unable to keep his thoughts from her, and Vence turned to him quickly, his creased brown face alight with interest.

"A good 'un?"

"A beauty. One of Jed Howarth's. Her name's Zara."

"I know that mare. She's worth a fortune. What did he take for her?" Vence was anxious. He knew as well

as Richard that money would only stretch so far, and if

they weren't selling their yearlings, they had very little income. Profit from the farm kept the stud. Just about. It was a losing battle. If only they sold the youngsters . . . but both Vence and Richard were horse crazy, and neither could bear to think of them being trained too soon and perhaps broken by being ridden in several races, their strength overtaxed. It wasn't right, and a horse wasn't grown till four. People rode them too young and bred them too young and then were surprised when they turned sickly on them, or, running their hearts out, willing as maybe, burst a blood vessel and died at the winning post.

But that was the way of the world. Everything for money, for quick results and a quick turnover. Some men were even breeding from their heifers a year early, reckoning that they were giving no return for their keep while they fed fat and didn't calve or give milk. Wonder was they let kids stay on at school till sixteen. The way things were, someone would suddenly reckon a lad could pay his way at twelve, and turn him out to work. World was mad, Vence concluded, eyeing the ram. Good beast that.

"Fifteen hundred guineas," Richard said. It sounded a lot of money but not when you considered that the average price at the last yearling sales at Newmarket was over two thousand guineas.

"For that mare?" Vence was incredulous. "He must be crazy. She's worth two thousand—or more."

"They say he's overstretched," Jack Braithwaite said. "Pushed for money on every side. Taxed to the hilt. Had to pay a hell of a lot of tax this year and that meant selling more than he'd intended. So it's said. He's got fourteen men and lads on that stud. That's a big wage bill. He's getting rid of some of 'em and cutting down t' number of mares. And he'd let you have his best . . . he knows she'll be cared for. Crazy about his beasts, is Jed."

Richard nodded.

They were both crazy. A man had no right to become fond of an animal when he bred it for profit, but both he and Jed were unable to remain cold-blooded about them. They all had their own ways and tricks and characters, and it was necessary not to get to know them too well if they were to be sold. That was easier said than done. He had always liked animals, and even the cows knew him and came to have their polls scratched.

One of the men was driving the cattle out into the lane. The grey cold light of first day chilled the landscape to bleakness. A sheepdog came out of the kennel and stretched and yawned, and then sat down and scratched vigorously. Nan Braithwaite came out to feed the hens, small, dark, and neat in jeans and anorak. The farm was waking to life. The gander joined the fowls and sent them scattering as he made for the food, and Nan grinned.

"Caingy steg," she said, mimicking old Adam, and the gander turned his head indignantly as if he understood that she had accused him of bad temper.

Richard and Jack went into the farmhouse. Built, like the Manor House, of solid stone, sheltered from the wind by trees and a high stone wall, it was an island of comfort. Nan had piled the fire high, and the flames welcomed them. The sheepdog followed them and went to his bowl to feed, and the big Persian cat, lying on the hearthrug, surrounded by her kittens, rolled onto her back and batted at them as they dodged about her and played with her lashing tail. One clawed too hard and she slapped him swiftly. He retreated, abashed, and sat watching her, as if unable to make up his mind just what crime had been his and afraid to try again lest he repeat his error. A few minutes later she walked over to him and, holding him down with her paw, began to wash him. Forgiven and at ease again, he purred loudly. His mother was privileged, a by-the-fire pet cat. Outside the other cats, half wild, kept down the mice and rats.

Nan poured coffee and took the bacon rashers from the Aga oven, where they had been put to keep hot. Richard always ate at the farmhouse, being up too early for those in his own home. It was a good part of the day, sitting at the big kitchen table, his plate heaped high with bacon and sausage and egg and tomatoes, the men about him talking farm talk, horse talk, tales of the dalesmen they knew and of the farms near by, gossiping about the last sale and the next sale and the rumor that Ben Sidebotham was selling up and retiring to live with his son in the South.

There was a rending crash and a yell from outside.

"Ram's loose."

Jack whistled the dog. The ram, brooding in his new home, hating strangers, wanting to be back among his kind, had charged the door. The bolt had splintered away from the wood, and he was free. Free to run across the yard, following the path that the cows had taken, through the gate that had not been closed, because Tom Witton was lazy and there was no stock in the yard, so why bother.

"Need another dog. Rip won't manage alone," Jack said and freed the bitch. She was penned away by herself, in season, and he didn't want pups. The dog would behave while he was working, Jack was sure of that. But after . . . it was a risk he had to take. He suspected that as soon as the ram was caught the dog and bitch would run off together. He hadn't another dog. Sweep

ZARA had been run over two days before, and there had not been time to replace him. Always something.

Rip, the sheepdog, ran into the lane. He knew his work, knew he had to turn the ram back towards the farm, and needed no more than Jack's first instruction of "Bring him in."

Pep, the bitch, waited behind, ready to nip at the ram's heels, pretending to bite. She knew better than to try in reality. She was delighted to be out of the run where she spent over three weeks each time she was in heat. She waited, lying ready, tail weaving from side to side.

Rip had come to the front of the ram and was barking at him. Bramble put his head down, ready to toss. He was not afraid of dogs. That could make things difficult, Jack thought sourly, running forward, intending to cut off the ram and grab his horns.

The milk lorry, turning into the lane, late, and driven by a new man, was going too fast. The driver saw the dog, saw the ram, saw the man running and swore violently, jamming on the brakes with all his strength. The lorry twisted and slid into the side of the road.

The ram was terrified by the sight of the lorry hurtling towards him, by the crash that followed, and by the furious yells of the driver.

"Hell's teeth," Richard said inadequately, as the ram streaked past him towards Pep, who ran at him barking. The beast was bewildered. His bravery had gone and he was once more a timid creature, forgetting the arrogance of his mature age and his horns. He wanted shelter, he wanted comfort, he wanted darkness. He wanted to be away from men and dogs and things of monstrous size that roared and crashed and fell.

44 He turned in at the gate and headed for his pen.

That had the merit of familiarity, and it was dark. Nan
pushed the door to and backed the car against it to
keep it shut.

"And Rip's run off with the bitch. That means pups,
and we soon won't be able to work Pep for a few weeks.
I'll have to get another dog. And one that's trained,
what's more. Hell of a nuisance losing Sweep."

"Poor Sweep," Nan said. She was fond of the dogs
and liked them in the house. They were company if
they were not being used and also good guard dogs.
There were strange callers on a farm, especially in summer, when hikers came out from the towns. Most of
them were sensible, but one or two had light fingers,
and one had frightened her badly. Proved to be out of
his mind, poor devil, but that hadn't helped at the
time. He'd threatened her with a stick, wanting her
money, and taken her by the throat, and Sweep had
jumped on him and bitten hard and then held on.
Nan didn't like remembering, even now. They had
come for him from a near-by Home, from which, it
seemed, he'd escaped. He was once more safely locked
up.

"I'd like a dog of my own," she said. "I don't like
being here alone when you've got both dogs."

Jack looked at her blankly and then suddenly remembered the previous year's scare.

"I'll get you a dog. A good big one," he promised.

"No rest for the wicked," Richard said, coming into the
yard. "Best get on. There's work to do."

He went across to the stud. Vence was busy grooming
the mares. The two lads were exercising foals, walking
them on a rope, teaching them to follow obediently.
One of the unschooled youngsters pulled back and
reared.

"That won't do." Richard spoke sharply but quietly,

not wanting to alarm the foal further. "Don't pull him. He'll come if you're gentle. Like this."

He took the rope and began to walk, talking to the little beast.

"That one's a lile nazzart," the stable lad said sullenly. "Got his own mind."

"It takes time, and patience. And he must trust you," Richard said. The foal was following obediently, trusting him completely. The lads weren't always gentle. No horse sense. Richard sighed.

"T' mare's coom."

The yell from the yard made Richard jump and the foal shied. The rope twisted from his hand, and the animal ran off.

"Damn," Richard said irritably. No use leaving him free. He had to learn, and now the youngster was scared he'd take some catching. And he wanted to go and look at the mare. He made a vow to give a dressing-down to the lad who had yelled. If only he could get the kind of men that his grandfather had had. Men who had grown up with horses and knew them as well as they knew themselves. It was getting more and more difficult. The lads wanted more money and they objected to work that was likely to go on till all hours, and if a horse was sick he or Vence or Jack had to do all the nursing. Couldn't ever be certain the lads would do it properly. Not even interested, these two. And not horse-wise either, but a pair of lads from farther north who had become redundant when the mine closed down. Not trained to anything.

"I'll catch the little un," Vence said. "Go and look to the mare."

Richard did not need telling again. He ran into the yard, where Jed's man was opening the horse-box. The mare cowered inside, terrified, never having left Jed's farm before. The blacksmith had always come to her,

and she had never been shown. She was trembling and
wet with sweat.

"Vence 'as kepped t' foal," old Adam said. He had
seen the horse-box come into the yard, looking out of
the window of his flat above the stable, and was curious. He decided that he felt better, although he had
an aching head. "Ah doan't trust t' lads. So Ah've coom
down."

"You'd be better in your bed." Richard's eyes were
on the mare.

"Come on then, pretty. No one'll hurt you." He held
out his hand, a sugar lump in it, but she backed away,
trembling. It was all too strange, and the smells were
unfamiliar, and there were other horses here, horses she
did not know and was afraid to meet. She backed again,
and a small head shoved determinedly from behind her,
as the donkey moved out of her way. He saw the sugar
and, being younger and trusting, stretched out his
head.

"You come on out first," Richard suggested, and the
tiny shaggy creature came towards him on delicate legs,
while the mare looked on, her ears flat on her head.

"T' donkey's mannerly," Adam said. He was watching the mare, as fascinated by her elegance as Richard
had been. "Eh, t' mare's fansome."

"Handsome as they come," Richard agreed. He did
not like her flattened ears. She promised trouble.

"Coom oop, pretty," the driver said, and held out his
hand. "You knaw me, then."

She came, walking distrustfully, testing the ramp of
the horse-box with each hoof before she put her weight
on it. Midnight, in his stable on the other side of the
yard, saw her and neighed a sudden greeting, and in a
moment she was dancing in panic and temper, and the
noise of her hooves on the wood terrified her.

Midnight called again. Most studs kept the stallions

away from the mares, but Richard felt that this was hard on them and that they were lonely and bored. He had always kept both his on the other side of the yard and had never had any difficulties. The mares were used to the stallions talking to them and answered back if they felt like it, and the foals were interested in the big black and the sleek bay. There was always something to watch, and unless they were being exercised, they stayed in sight and sound of the busy men, enjoying their company. Both hated being alone. It made them more biddable, being used to the men.

She was more beautiful than he remembered. She was glorious. She was the realization of a dream, perfection on four legs. Mane and tail gleamed in a shaft of sun that angled into the box; her sleek shining coat rippled as she moved her head. Nostrils flared, ears alert, she watched him suspiciously.

Even the two stable lads were looking at her admiringly.

"I'll kill the lad that harms or scares her. With my own hands," Richard said.

Adam was coughing, fit to burst his heart, but he had come nearer, unable to take his eyes off her. Nobody knew how old the man was. He had been stud groom for more years than Richard could remember, born and bred among horses, knowing their ways. The rumour was that Adam was reared on mare's milk. He should have retired long ago, but had protested that he'd be dowly away from fowk and he wor as lish as ivver he was, and well able to carry on wi' wark. Now he was farm foreman, and helped, when free, with the stud.

Better able than some, Richard often thought. No stamina in modern lads. Nothing but skylarking and fooling, and he was tired of trying to find one who would do a day's work for a day's pay. He watched Adam.

The old man was moving towards the mare as if he were iron drawn by a magnet.

"Thee's fansome," he was saying. "Aaaaahh."

Words failed him. He walked towards her, hand held low, his breath hissing softly between his teeth. She watched him, focusing both eyes forwards, ears pricked towards him, head alert and interested. He offered no harm, and his gentle approach was reassuring.

She bent her head and sniffed at his outstretched hand. It smelled warm and familiar, of stables and horse hides and oats, of hay and of bran; there was faint background whiff of the stallion and a scent of the foals. And a rank smell of Adam that did not bother her at all. It merely identified him and would make him easily recognizable. She huffed at him, trusting him, and he moved towards her, closer now, and breathed into her nostrils, an old trick that he swore made a horse know you were its friend.

She moved towards him, and his hand went up to her neck, and he stroked her gently.

"Coom on, pretty," he said coaxingly. Magically, horse nuts appeared out of his pocket, and she stretched her head towards them and took them gently from his hand.

"She's gey mannerly," he said approvingly. A mannerly horse was well trained, treated right, and easy to handle in field or stable. She followed him, scarcely noticing that she was coming down the ramp of the horsebox, treading across the yard and into the loose box that was prepared for her.

"Trust Adam," Jack Braithwaite said. "He can handle any beast that's born. She went like a lamb."

Richard followed them into the stable. He held out his own hand, and she sniffed at him, finding here again the smell of other horses, a safe smell, a right smell. She breathed deeply and looked about her at the spacious loose box. There was a hay bag, high on the wall, easy to pull at, but safely hung to make sure she did not catch her legs in it. Richard could not wait to show her to the stallion, but it was not yet time. She could not be mated for three or four months yet. Almost three years before he could see her foal grown to safety, old enough to fend for itself. It would take a lot of keep before he got results. The worry that had niggled all night flared to a pitch that made him feel sick. He stroked the smooth golden neck and relaxed. The mare was worth it.

"Stay with her, Adam, and make sure she's easy," he said and turned out into the yard. It had been peaceful in the stable. If only he could stay there—but there were other things to do.

He went to look at the black stallion. Midnight was watching the yard, interested in the day's affairs and eager for conversation. Beside his stable, ears drooping, stood the little donkey, a bewildered expression on its face.

"Horse-box driver left him," one of the lads said. "Says t' mare won't settle wi' out t' donkey."

Richard nodded absently. His wife's curtains were drawn back. She would soon be down, possibly wanting her hunter saddled. He wished that she wouldn't ride. She vented her temper on the horse and Tarzan played her up as a result, so that she made matters worse by whipping him. It was a good job horses rarely turned on their riders, or Stella would come a cropper. He went to see if the hunter was ready for riding.

"I dunno." Paddy O'Hara was the only man he could trust to supervise in his absence, when Vence and Adam were not there. "Looks to me as if Tarzan's lame. Honest to God, it's a strange thing. There's not a swelling on him, nor a sign of heat in that off fore, but every time I put the saddle on him he favours that leg. Not the first time either. Whenever Mrs. Proud wants to go riding, these last few weeks, he's shown lameness in one leg or the other. It's a very funny thing."

Richard looked at the horse. He had heard of other beasts that feigned lameness. One of them had been a Windsor Grey that limped every time he was brought out to take his place in harness to pull the royal coach. He had been cured of his trick. Probably only one of those stories that went the rounds, but then there had been his own pony, Mustard.

He grinned to himself. Mustard had always gone lame when Richard's cousin wanted to ride. John had been very fat and had had hands that tore at the pony's mouth, and Mustard had put on such a good act that he fooled everyone. Except Richard, who had discovered that the pony was perfectly sound as soon as his cousin had gone. Artful as costers, were horses.

"Let me try him," he said, and tested the girths.

"Very funny," he told the horse, as he tightened the band a couple of notches. "Blew yourself out properly today, didn't you? You'd better watch that, Paddy. My wife doesn't always think to test the girths herself, and she might have an accident."

As if I'd care, Paddy thought sourly.

"Goes well enough," he said, dismounting, and bent to examine the foreleg. The hunter stood patiently. A moment later, he moved backwards, his ears flattening.

Stella was walking across the yard towards him. She was immaculate in her riding clothes, except that she had inexplicably tied a bright orange chiffon scarf at the throat of her jacket.

It was an effort to walk towards the men. Her head ached, as it did so often these days, and she felt more like staying in bed than going out riding. But she had never given in to bad health and she was not starting now. She needed exercise. Fresh air would cure her headaches, and then she would not need to drink so much to dull the pain.

Pain that made her so irritable, that made her lash out with her tongue at Sue and Richard, that badgered her until she could not control herself, but could only watch appalled and helpless, while her actions betrayed her. Today, she would make a real effort and be nice to Richard.

The pain stabbed her again. She was not giving in to it.

The hunter moved again.

"Stand," Richard said.

"Thank you," his wife said mockingly, coming over to the horse. "I didn't think you'd act as groom today. I'm honoured."

Richard straightened, wondering if the hunter really was trembling, or if he had imagined it.

"Paddy thinks Tarzan's lame," he said.

"Paddy should give up thinking," Stella answered. "He'll make the brute as lazy as he is himself. He's always trying to find some excuse for me not to ride. Paddy had better have another think. I'm not giving up one of my few pleasures because of a stupid horse."

She gathered the reins and flicked the whip across the horse's neck. He turned, obedient, and walked out through the gate which one of the lads had raced to open. It did not do to keep Stella waiting. He moved back from the gate as she rode through.

"You see," Paddy said. Tarzan was walking awkwardly, as if afraid to trust his weight on the off fore.

Richard did not answer. He was sure the horse was playing up and he knew why. He wished he could stop his wife riding. She had no sense.

Stella rode off, her hands trembling. She was miserably conscious of utter defeat. Perhaps, if she rode fast,
she could outpace the devils that drove her. Her heels
kicked at the hunter's sides, and Tarzan quickened his
pace.

Richard went to look at the mare. He would not be
able to keep away. She was his beauty, his future, his
life. She turned to him and dipped her head to his
hand and took the lump of sugar he offered. It was not
a habit he would encourage, but it would help to en-
dear him to her while they were getting to know one
another.

"Sell her soul for sweeties, would Zara. Like some
women," Paddy said laughing, and Richard, already
rubbed raw, wondered if he too were commenting on
Stella.

CHAPTER *four*

Sometimes during the following year Richard wondered if that day had marked a turning point in his life, if his purchase of the mare had set the pattern for the ill luck that was to dog him. Nothing, after that, seemed to go right. The day ended eventfully.

Chris arrived during the afternoon, in a mood of sullen resentment. A few moments later Stella strode into the yard, enraged, having been tossed from her hunter over a gate and into the mud beyond.

She arrived filthy and furious, the horse limping behind her, the mark of her slash on his neck. Richard, rarely bad-tempered, raged at her, broke her whip across his knee, and took the horse from her.

"It's the last time you ride," he said. He was white with anger, beyond himself with fury, unable, as ever, to bear the thought of one of his animals being hurt because of human stupidity.

"In future the men will have orders not to saddle your horse for you. You are not riding again."

She stared at him, wanting to shout back at him, wanting to vent on him all her spite and all her boredom, her need for a life of her own, life in a city with fun and bright lights and men to pay her the compliments and chivalries that she thought necessary to civilized existence. Instead she was shut away in the Dales, in bleak wintry weather or dreary summer, dependent for her needs on the whims of a lot of stupid horses, with men who could never think or talk anything but horse talk. Tears suddenly forced themselves down her cheeks, and she turned away, aware that the lads were staring at her and afraid that Richard might break his own rule and hit her. She had never seen him so angry.

If only she could control herself. She had had no intention of making such a scene. She had been cold, tired, and shaken after falling, and somehow, as always these days, her emotions overwhelmed her. Nothing ever went right, and Richard and Sue hated her. She had seen it in their eyes.

She shut the door behind her and stood for a moment in the cool quiet hall, trying to control her shaking body. There was a decanter on the sideboard. She poured herself a half glass of brandy, telling herself this would treat the shock from which she was obviously suffering.

She poured a second—and a third, and when the bitter edge of reality was blurred and dull she went upstairs to bathe and change. For the rest of the day she carried in her mind a nagging guilt and a vision of Richard's furious and uncomprehending expression.

Life was an aching pain that could barely be tolerated. She was no use to anyone. She sat, watching the dark creep over the Dales, a full glass ready to her hand, while slow tears spilled from her eyes and splashed unheeded.

She could never explain—and Richard would never understand.

As a result the mare was installed and taken for granted without any further comment. Stella took even less interest than before in what went on in the stables, and she spent as much as a week at a time away from them, ostensibly with her sister, although Richard, had he thought, did not really believe that. He no longer cared.

Slowly, as autumn crept on towards Christmas, Chris became part of the stables. He learned to approach the horses gently so that they trusted him, and he learned, very quickly, that although Zara was mild-tempered and biddable, she became terrified if anyone came up to her roughly: twice, when he had thoughtlessly gone into her loose box swinging a bucket, she reared and hit her head on the rafters, cutting the skin. Richard's sharp words and Vence's anger soon ensured that no one came to the mare without taking care not to alarm her.

Richard had never known any creature so gentle. She was spirited and lively, and loved to run, matching herself against the colts, chasing her shadow across the paddock, kicking up her heels in excitement on a blustery day, defying the wind, always wanting to lead, to be in front of the field, and she was no longer afraid of any of the other horses. She exacted her due from them, and they let her come first to the gate, knowing that if they did not, her quick teeth would nip them. She was not standing any nonsense from other animals. She had settled quickly and she was regal, entitled to her place as queen.

Wherever she went the donkey followed her. Sue was enchanted by him, and when they visited Jed's stud one afternoon and found his wife already breeding the beasts, with two dainty in-foal jennies both stabled in the yard, Sue asked Nan Braithwaite at the farm to find her a jenny too. She used all the money she had in the bank to buy Velvet, and now there were two donkeys in the field to act as courtiers to Zara.

Zara had given her allegiance to Richard. She came to the gate to watch for him when she knew that he was due. She stood still for him, as for nobody else, when she cut her leg on a bucket as she backed in alarm when a strange dog came chasing into the yard. She was bitterly jealous of the farm dogs that sometimes followed at his heels, and she did her best to prevent any other horse coming to him for fussing when he came to the paddock and she was free.

Each morning she vied with Midnight in calling for his attention. She knew his footsteps and was waiting eagerly, and greeted him by dropping her warm tongue into the palm of his hand. He shook it gently and laughed at her, and she rubbed her head up and down his clean shirt, leaving dark marks on it, so that he invariably had to change after he had attended to her needs.

Only Adam was greeted with anything like the same feeling. Paddy she tolerated. She invariably played up Chris and the stable lads, moving when they asked her to stand, and suddenly obstinate if they wished to come to her manger, blocking the way.

When they complained to Richard she showed him how absurd they were, obeying him instantly, eyeing him with love, shifting obediently as he asked her, saying plainly with her enormous brown eyes that she could never misbehave, the lads were inventing it.

"Lads need a good fliting," Adam said one day, when there had been more complaints than usual. "Mare's kysty. That's t' trooble."

"She's fussy all right," Sue said one afternoon, when she had taken Zara into the stable out of the rain. "She hates being wet. I dried her, and every time I stopped rubbing she tried to dry herself on me. I'm completely exhausted."

She laughed up at Richard. Stella had been away for

three days and the house was an easier place without her. Nan came across from the farmhouse each morning and helped Mrs. Batt, from the village, to tidy and clean, and Sarah Vence cooked for them. Her meals were mouth-watering, and Sue did them full justice. Even Chris was losing his drawn appearance and filling out. His limp was lessening, and the hard work in the stables seemed to be good for him. Away from his parents, he was becoming a different person. Richard enjoyed his company and Chris revelled in the horses. He had no liking for an academic life, to his father's sorrow.

He spent the first three days fretting, until Vence suddenly lost his temper and produced a tirade of words that made Chris hot to remember.

"Think you're hard done by?" Vence had said. "Well, you're spoiled. Spoiled rotten and mollycoddled. There's men wi' much worse troubles than you doing a good day's work. Dunno what makes you think you're so special. No time for your sort, and don't you forget it. If lads want to stare at you walking around sorry for yourself, then they can stare. I won't stop 'em. You can stop 'em by not limping around as if end of world were nigh. Just get on wi' living, and remember I don't hold wi' no slacking, not from you or anyone else either. And if you want to fight lads for looking at you then fight. I won't help. I hope they knock some sense into your stupid head."

Chris had raged all morning, resenting Vence bitterly, and later come to blows with Dick Holroyd, who had knocked him down and then laughed at him.

"I'll do that every time you growl at me, and that's fair warnin'," he said. Tom Witton stood and grinned at them.

Chris got up resentfully. Someone in his father's

school would have interfered and prevented his being hurt. After all, he'd been so ill he'd nearly died.

That affected nobody at the Proud stud. Richard ignored his tantrums, and within a month it was not worth giving way to them. They had no effect on anybody. Not even Sue, who laughed at him and teased him and when he limped badly, trying, she was sure, to attract attention, called him Old Lagleg and talked about centipedes with wooden legs. She enjoyed having him there. It would have been fun to have a brother.

Soon Chris was exercising Tarzan and enjoying the feel of a horse between his legs. There was a paddock beyond the house where Sue jumped her pony, practising for the summer shows, and where Richard trained the young colts, and here Chris and Tarzan went every day. The exercise was strengthening his muscles. Chris was sleeping at night, and his temper was easier.

"Zara may be kysty," Chris said. "But I wish she wouldn't play me up."

"She knows you expect her to." Richard was filling his pipe, concentrating on the job in hand. His study looked untidy and comfortable without Stella to come in twice daily and reduce it to perfect order. Her need for tidiness had become an obsession. She could not bear anything out of line or out of place, and she hated dirty ashtrays. Only when she had friends in for one of her parties, and five or six drinks inside her, did she ever relax.

"I've written a poem for school homework," Sue said. She was sitting at the table, her legs tucked under her, her dark hair untidy from her fingers that always rummaged through it when she was working. Chris was stretched out on the settee and Pru, the Siamese, knowing that Stella was not around, had followed them indoors and was lying in front of the fire.

"Cor, brains," Chris said lazily. "Bet it's lousy."

"You're not going to read it," Sue said.

"Like to bet?" He reached out a long arm and grabbed the paper.

"Give it back, you beast." Sue went to get it, but Chris held her off.

"It's not bad. Hey, Mr. Proud. Listen. No, shut up, Sue, I'm serious."

He began to read.

"Horses . . .
Running on the plains,
With flying tails and tossing manes.
Their wise brown eyes view the skies.
Their coats are wet from the summer rains.
They like to roll
Where the grass is cool beneath their hooves,
And then they sleep.
And wake again to feed and run
And bask beneath the midday sun.
Hear thunder of the fleetfoot herds,
The winging wonder of the birds,
See flowers with petals dewy bright . . .
Then darkness—
And the star-crazed night."

"Not at all bad," Chris said.

"You're joking. I can't get it right. I've been working on it for a week," Sue said despairingly. "I wish I could take exams in horsemanship instead of English. I'm hopeless at it."

"It's not bad at all," Richard said. He took the paper from Chris. "It needs tidying and rethinking, perhaps, but it's got something."

He stopped. Stella's car had skidded to a standstill in the yard. They looked at one another, uneasy.

"Oh, Pru, it's a fair cop," Sue said softly and the Siamese, hearing Stella's key in the door and her footsteps in the hall, looked distractedly about the room for sanctuary, and then, ears flattened on her head, raced to Richard and leaped into his arms, clinging desperately to the rough tweed coat, leaning against him, her eyes wild.

"Oh, my God," Richard said under his breath as the door opened.

He knew the signs. Stella had been drinking. It was a miracle she ever got home safely. Then he saw the man behind her, neat, dapper, dark-haired, and small, with a thin line of moustache and dark olive skin and bright eyes that were vivid with amusement.

"You know I won't have that damned cat in here," Stella said, picking on the first thing that came into her sight. She aimed a slap at Pru, and Richard turned sideways so that he caught the blow. The cat leaped from his arms and raced out of the room. The front door was shut, and Pru cried to be let out.

Sue ran towards the door, but her mother caught her arm.

"You needn't go. What have you been up to? Look at you. It's nice to have a daughter, isn't it? Spotty face and hair that looks as if you've been romping with a tiger. A daughter to be proud of . . . like her father. Pity you aren't horses, all of you. And what the hell are you doing here?" she added to Chris. "Thought you were Vence's lodger. I won't have stable boys in the house." Stella's voice was high and her tone venomous.

Chris flushed, not sure what he ought to do or say. Richard put a hand on his shoulder.

"Why don't you make yourself a cup of coffee, Stella?" he asked.

"Coffee? Susan can make it. My dearest little pretty

daughter can greet her mother properly. Look at her staring. Can't even kiss me. And what's that you're holding so tightly, Stable Boy?"

She reached over and grabbed the paper from Chris, tearing the corner.

"My God. Writing poetry to horses now. This whole family's mental."

She tore the paper across and across into smaller and smaller pieces. Sue watched her numbly.

"I haven't even got a copy," she wailed.

"I suppose your boy friend wrote it for you as a love lyric. Oh, God, why did I ever come home?"

She turned and went out of the room. The man who had followed her looked at Richard.

"I thought I'd better see her safely home," he said uncertainly. "I drove her car . . . if you have any transport . . ."

"I'll get a man to drive you." Richard picked up the phone that communicated with the stables. Paddy was free.

The man was no longer amused. He had, at first, thought Stella was fun and this trip a bit of a joke, but what he had seen convinced him he wanted nothing more to do with her, or with any of them. He couldn't get away fast enough. He left, to wait outside in the porch. Nobody followed him.

Stella, who had gone upstairs, leaned against her bedroom door, feeling sick. Dear God, what's wrong with me, she wondered. She walked to the window and stared blindly over the Dale.

The Weere trickled, silver cool, through the shallows.

Sarah, who had heard her come in and had come over to the house, tapped on the door.

"Bed for you, love," she said, matter-of-fact as always, and when Stella dropped onto a chair, sobbing uncontrollably, her arms were ready, and her voice as gentle as when she comforted a sick animal. She patted Stella's shoulder and looked in her turn out at the murmuring Weere, and wondered what was happening to all of them. She had tried advice—now she could only stand by, and be there when she was needed.

Sue sat with tears trickling under her closed eyelids. Chris had clenched his fists, not daring to look at Richard. Richard had gone into the hall where he had heard Pru wail in anguish. Stella had stamped her foot at the cat as she had passed her. Pru hated being stamped at.

Silently Richard lifted her and went towards the stables. He saw Chris lean over and take Sue's hand, and the pair of them went off together. Sometime he would have to face up to the situation, but he did not know what to do or how to do it.

Paddy brought the Morris, and the stranger climbed in, with an awkward nod of farewell. Paddy had seen Stella come home and his face was carefully and stonily bleak. He did not even glance at Richard. It was not the first time there had been a scene and it would not be the last. Every word that Stella had said had been audible outside.

Vence was sweeping the yard, a task that the boys always did. He had heard Stella's voice, and anger was riding him, so that he had to use activity to prevent himself from exploding. Beyond him, Adam was filling a bucket and muttering to himself under his breath.

There was nothing any of them could do.

Richard entered the stable and stood holding the cat. The Siamese was trembling. All the animals were afraid of Stella. He sighed, looking out across the yard. He put Pru down and she streaked to the cottage for sanctuary.

There was no sanctuary for Richard.

He took the brush and began to groom Zara, who submitted gracefully, pleased to find that she was having extra and unexpected attention, even though it was the wrong time of day.

An hour later, her coat was shining, her mane and tail were gleaming silk, and she was restive. The brushing had soothed the man.

He sat on the manger and looked at the mare.

She was beauty incarnate, gentle and good-tempered. She was consolation. He did not want to leave her. He moved her so that he could clean the stable himself, lose himself in work, find satisfaction in attending to her needs.

He bedded her, forking the straw thick and even, and then went into the feed room and measured the feeds. Vence brought him coffee, but said nothing.

He drank it, and long after the men had gone home he sat in the dark stable, savouring the quiet, listening to the horses' breathing, the rustle of movement, the sounds of approaching night.

The stable cat came back to her kittens and nosed his shoe, and accepted his presence. Vence returned twice, but did not know what to say, and finally left him sitting alone in the dark. Sue and Chris had gone to find comfort in Sarah's kitchen and Sarah's prosaic talk and her deliberate ways.

It was very late when Richard locked the stable. Sarah was waiting with food for him, but he had no desire to eat.

He took his stick and walked past the cottage and down the lane. The moors stretched in front of him, lit by a glimmer from a moonslip riding the rags of clouds.

Richard walked down to the Weere, and stood by the light-specked water, and listened to the sound of the river thrusting among the stones. Owlcall in the distance chided him with cowardice, and some small animal slipped from the water at his feet, startling him to brief awareness.

He sat on a rock, his mind deliberately blank. He filled his pipe and listened to the loneliness, knowing that the moors were less barren than his own life, and the darkness was less desolate than he.

CHAPTER *five*

Sam Lethwaite had not been born; he had happened. Annie Lethwaite, who was big and bouncing and generous, had never been able to plan her life. Not until Sam's advent.

Her mother was dead, and her father, no angel himself where women were concerned, had heard the news stolidly.

"Ye can keep t' bairn," he said. "But only one, mind. Unless ye find yerself a man to keep you. Ah'm not fillin' t' house wi' your byblows."

Having Sam made a difference. He needed food and he needed clothes, and this took more money than Annie would have believed possible in her feckless days.

She went to work in the laundry in the near-by town, leaving early each morning, and returning at six to more household chores and to knitting for Sam.

Sam was left at Dora Lee's house each day, along with the other babies that needed minding. Most of the men in Keyburn worked on the land, and farming didn't bring in enough to hold body and belly together, not even with overtime. The wives went out to work too, some on the farms, others working in the many guest houses in the summer and doing as best they could in the winter.

Dora might be rough and ready, but she was well-intentioned and trustworthy. She paddled the children's bottoms when they misbehaved, dealt with real wickedness with a lusty clout on the ear, made sure that they ate their sandwiches, made them a drink of strong dark tea that scalded their mouths when they drank it, and yelled at them not to go down near the water.

By the time Sam was five he knew a great deal about protecting himself from bullies, about keeping out of mischief, and, more to the point, about not being found out. He could dress himself without help and could count to ten, and he knew enough to stay comfortably ahead in class without overworking when he started school.

But he was small.

Annie could not understand it. Her father was over six feet tall with shoulders and a head on him like the big bull up at the Proud place, where old Aaron worked on the farm.

She herself was large, more than ample where it mattered most, so that she was often the butt of jokes among the men when she went up with Aaron's lunch on a Saturday. She teased them back with good-humoured laughter, but none of them came near her. Her life belonged to Sam and he was all-important, a clever lad who needed a chance, and he was going to get it. No one had offered marriage, and she wasn't having another bairn to feed. It couldn't be done. Sam was the wages of sin and not such a bad wage at that, but she wasn't falling again. Not for anyone.

Sam filled any blank there might have been in her life, and work filled the rest, but she worried about his size. The doctor, when Annie wanted to know why he was so small, asked about his father.

Annie shrugged.

"There were one or two little men . . ." she said. She did not remember clearly, and the doctor preferred not to pursue the subject.

Sam remained small, but he was tough enough and brave enough to stand up to boys much bigger than he, and he soon cured them of bullying him by waiting until they turned away and then grabbing them from behind, holding their elbows in a grip that could not be loosened. His hard little head butted into their backs until they felt sick. After that, they left him alone.

He did not need minding after he was five. When school ended he wandered along the forbidden river bank, watching the trout lying almost motionless under the water, the current washing over their backs. He paddled barefoot and waded out to the island where he climbed the trees and came home dirty and wet, with torn clothes, and Annie tutted, while old Aaron grinned and said, inevitably, "Lads will be lads, and better so."

Sam learned to run for cover when Aaron came home on a Saturday night, roaring verses from the Psalms, stumbling over the plank into the cottage that nudged the humpback bridge across the Weere, yelling for Annie.

"Man is evil," he thundered, and Annie hastily jerked her head and sent Sam away, and he lay in the tiny room under the rafters on his lumpy bed, listening to Aaron ranting and raging until the yells dropped to a mutter and he heard the old man staggering up the stairs, his weight on Annie, who undressed him and put him to bed, still bellowing "Man that is born of woman is born to sorrow."

Nor was it ever wise to talk next morning, for his grandfather sat at the breakfast table morose as the old gander down the road at Broken Wall Farm, and drank strong tea, and muttered about the fate of those who frequented Sodom and Gomorrah.

"Look not on the wine when it is red," was always one of his phrases on Sunday morning. Later, he dressed in his best black suit and went to church, where he prayed for salvation and vowed never to drink again. A vow that he had broken every Saturday as long as Sam could remember.

On one of these Sundays Sam wandered farther along the river than usual, and for the first time, he saw a pure-bred horse. He knew other horses, of course; the little ponies that trotted gaily, pulling the ragmen's carts; the big Dales ponies that the farmers rode when they overlooked the sheep. Ponies were easier to manage than anything else on the hillsides. Surefooted and sturdy, and cheaper to keep than a vehicle, since they grazed along with the cattle and needed little extra save hay in winter. No pampering for them.

This was not a Dales cob or a pony. This was Jed Howarth's Arab stallion, magnificent and moody, pacing in his paddock on the other side of the river. Sam had never seen such a horse. He sat and looked and felt that he would burst if he could not touch it. He had to feel the bones under the shining skin, had to ride on its back.

He waded the river, which sparkled over the boulders and was never higher than his knees.

No one was about. He looked towards the stables and the stone house high on the hill, and he held out his hand for the stallion to sniff. He was eight years old and the horse towered over him, looking down at him with brown eyes and an unfathomable expression.

Sam touched the horse gently, slid his hands along

the warm neck, and then, with a swift movement, was onto Rajah's back. The stallion was startled and out-raged. He bucked in fury, but Sam grabbed his mane and hung on, excited beyond anything that he had ever known.

Rajah turned and raced round the field and bucked again. Sam held on tightly, but he was not prepared for the stallion to rear and squeal and lash out at the air with his forelegs. He slid off backwards. Rajah relaxed and began to crop the grass. Sam stroked him thought-fully. One day, he promised himself . . .

Meanwhile he was once more wet and dirty and had a massive bruise on his side that he could see blue and coming black and yellow at the edges, and Annie would be wild with him. He trotted off home.

After that he haunted the stables. He came when school ended and helped Jed's men, and because he was small and impish and amusing they tolerated him and teased him and let him muck out the stalls where the foals were kept, and let him fill the buckets with water.

One memorable day, the day of his tenth birthday, one of the men lifted him onto a saddled horse and showed him how to sit, how to hold the reins, how to tell the horse to move.

As Sam rode round the yard he suddenly realized that this was what he had been born for, this was what he was waiting for, this was the meaning of his whole existence.

"Boy's a natural," one of the men said, and after that Sam was allowed to exercise the quieter horses, walking them round the yard, proud on their backs, looking down on men who normally towered above him.

By the time he was fourteen he knew he was going to be a jockey. He hitchhiked whenever he could to the race meetings at Wetherby and watched the elite of the horse world riding. He knew every rider by name. He

could tell you which man rode a fine flashy finish with
his whip flailing, and which rode still as a trout on a
summer day, only moving at the last as he quickened
his mount, and brought his horse time and again to the
winning post.

He knew their names and their weights and their
wins and their losses. He knew who had a chipped
elbow and who had a broken collarbone. He knew
which trainer could put a good jockey on a strange
horse and bring him in a winner, without fail, and he
knew which stables were likely to win most races.

He knew all this by listening and watching, making
mental notes, never thinking to read a newspaper or realizing that his heroes would figure there. He watched
the paddock as the horses paced by, memorizing the
shape and look of the winners, seeking some reason for
this horse to run better than that. Observing before a
race that one of the mares was favouring, very slightly,
her off fore, or that a horse that had never worn blink-
ers was suddenly wearing them. He learned to put
two and two together, and could often pick out the
three places before each race.

He wanted to ride. He needed to ride. On a horse he
experienced a wild excitement, a savage exultation, the
knowledge that he could make the beast go where he
wished, do as he wanted. It was an exhilaration beyond
anything he had ever experienced, and his need was
desperate, blinding him to everything else. He spent
every spare second with the horses. He haunted Jed's
stud, but there was no room for an extra boy. Jed's men
were serious men who wished to learn all they could,
perhaps to go on and train horses themselves, perhaps
to work in one of the big Newmarket stables. They had
their sights set on the future. Jed paid well, and he
only wanted the best.

In other parts of the year he had young veterinary

students helping, also learning about horses. Sam could help as much as he liked, but there was no job with a wage attached waiting for him. He had to take a job in the supermarket in the town where his mother worked, and he hated every moment of the day.

He was almost seventeen when Richard Proud bought Zara.

Sam had known her since she was foaled, had loved her beyond anything in the world, and at times, when nobody knew and she was hidden by the trees that clumped together at the end of the paddock, he had ridden her, bareback, revelling in the feel of her. She learned to look for him, to come and greet him, and she returned his affection, so that when she was sold he went home sullen, and sat in gloom the whole evening.

In his dreams he owned her, he raced her against every horse in the land, he brought her to victory, never needing more than a touch on her neck to bring out the latent stride that would send them up from the back of the field to the front in one glorious burst of speed.

"What's oop wi' you, then?" Aaron asked irritably after he had told Sam three times to pass the salt.

"Cat's got 'is tongue," Annie said. She ruffled her son's fair hair, a gesture that Sam hated. He straightened it with his fingers and glared at her.

"They've sold Zara," he said forlornly.

"Jed's mare? Not gone far, lad. Proud's got her up t' stables."

Aaron stuffed his mouth full of cheese and pickles and champed his way through the meal. Sam could scarcely bear to sit still. His appetite had gone. He wanted to see the mare, to see that she was safe and that she was settled and that she had good stabling. She was used to the best. Would they be kind to her, he won-

dered? Jed insisted on kindness, but Sam knew nothing
of Richard Proud.

"Get off wi' ye, boy," Aaron said. "Like sitting wi' a
badger wi' t' itch under its tail."

Sam was off and out through the door. If he was
quick he might get a lift from the landlord of the Bell,
who drove a lorry by day and was home to help his wife
open up in the evening. He always left the village green
about teatime.

Jim Oxton was climbing into the cab.

"Coom oop, lad," he said, and gave Sam a hand. "Little but good, eh?" He winked.

Sam grinned dutifully. Everyone seemed to make the
same remark, and his grandfather sometimes looked at
him and commented that beer tasted as good in half
pints as in pints. It was a well-worn joke.

Sam slipped into the yard. The mare was in her stall,
and she greeted him at once. Nobody was about. He
stroked her and gentled her and looked about him curiously.

He heard footsteps and slipped away. He did not
want to be found. Nobody here knew him. He begged a
lift from the village policeman, who lived in a cottage
just down the road from Sam's own home. Tom Barnet
did not mind. He liked to know the lads and exchange
a few words with them, and a friendly warning would
sometimes keep them out of greater mischief than the
minor peccadillo that he had just uncovered. The village lads liked him, and he knew how to jolly them
along, laughing at them and teasing them.

"Going to be a jockey, are you, Sam?" he asked now,
as he drove the car expertly down the winding dusk-
filled lanes.

"I'd like that," Sam said wistfully. "Don't even know
how t' start."

"Get a job in t' Proud place and mebbe they'll help you," Tom suggested. "I'll have a word wi' them. Would you like that? They need a really good lad— both their lads are leaving. Too much work with horses."

Sam nodded, liking the idea too much to be able either to put his feelings into words or to believe that such an event would ever come to pass. Wishes only came true in kids' tales.

Tom was as good as his word, and Sam found himself stable lad at the Proud stud. He talked to Sue and helped her with her donkeys, and Richard was amused at the way the mare watched for the boy and greeted him eagerly when he came into the yard.

Sam soon learned that Stella was rarely about the place, and when he did see her, he was startled by her beauty. She was small and dark, with perfect features and hair with the same sheen as the hide of the bay stallion that was kept as a teaser. She moved like a racehorse, and Sam had never seen such wonderful clothes or such startling colours. Stella, on the rare occasions on which they met, sensed his admiration and was entertained by it and rewarded him with one of her rare smiles, which made him her slave for life, no matter what they said about her. When she chose, she could enchant people. But these days she rarely had enough energy and interest to bother.

Vence, talking in the Bell to Jed's head man, discovered that Sam could ride and put him up on one of the horses. He watched him curiously. The boy had a style all his own. He had an understanding of the need of the horse, and, as he rode, the two of them were more than partners. They were fused. Vence took them to the field which Sue used for schooling her jumpers, and Sam and his mount flowed together in a movement

that was almost incredible. If the horse faltered the boy
knew by instinct how to correct him. If the horse was
right, Sam let him have his head, left him to decide
how to jump, so that at each fence the horse stood well
back and swept over in an easy beautiful fluid movement that had Vence in an ecstascy of admiration.

"There's only one man ever rode like that," he commented to Sarah that night as they lay in bed. "Dick
Trailer. Remember him? A likely lad from down south
. . . came up for Wetherby races and used to stop over
often enough. Courting Annie at one time, we thought,
and then he was killed in a plane crash, taking a horse
to France. Reckon . . ."

"You don't reckon nothing," Sarah said. "Least said,
soonest mended, and won't help anyone to let cat out o'
bag now."

"You knew . . ." Vence said accusingly.

"Aye. Saw t' likeness long ago, but it won't help
Annie. What's dead is best left buried, and mebbe she
don't know for sure. She were as bad as her dad when
she were younger. Been a mortal good mother to t' lad
all same, and no hanky panky since he were born."

"Once bit . . ." Vence said.

"We could put him up on the mare as an apprentice
—and race her before she gets a foal," he said next
morning.

Richard Proud was doubtful.

"He's had no training with horses," he said.

"He's got an instinct." Vence answered. "Come and
watch him ride. And Jed's men taught him—he's had
some teaching—Jed only has the best—"

Sam was exercising Zara, who now loved him beyond
anyone in the stables. She greeted him in the morning
with a frantic whinny, and he spent as much of his time
as he could spare with her, eager to serve her and envy-

ing Richard and Paddy, who between them catered to
her every need. He had never loved any creature so
much in his life.

When Vence let him ride her, he was unable to
speak. He had not believed that he would ever, legiti-
mately, be allowed on her back, but Vence knew that
Sam's delicate hands would not harm her mouth, that
his easy ways would teach her all she needed to know at
present without frightening her, and that the perfect
trust she had in him would benefit both of them. She
was never completely at ease with anyone else. She was
a wayward little mare, sensitive, hating undue noise or
any sort of roughness. She had a temper which she
showed at times, especially if she was ignored or neg-
lected in favour of other horses. If Richard spoke to
Midnight her hoof caught the stable door in sharp
anger, and if Sam passed her without a word, she
kicked again. It was one habit that was hard to break,
although Vence had tried every trick he knew to cure
her, lest she damage herself by her temper.

Sam circled the field. He took her gently, encourag-
ing her to learn, and when she had walked and trotted
for thirty minutes and loosened her muscles, he took
her down the lane of jumps. Just once, every day,
Vence had said, and where his wonderful mare was concerned, Sam always obeyed. He bent over her as they
approached the first fence and stroked her neck and
spoke to her, and she began to canter. Richard watched
the pair of them approach the fence and leap over it,
and the boy settled in his saddle and sent her on, and
up, and over, on, and up, and over, never putting a foot
wrong, soaring and landing in an easy glorious fluidity
of movement that was more like flying than riding.

"By Heaven, you're right," Richard said. "I've only,
ever, seen one man ride like that. And he's dead. Been

dead for sixteen years, I reckon. Used to come up . . .
how old's Sam?"

"Seventeen soon. Dick's been dead for over sixteen years. And dead men tell no tales." Vence was stroking his chin thoughtfully.

"Maybe not. But they sometimes leave telltales behind them, it seems. . . . We've got to encourage that boy. Give him a chance. You can't waste that kind of inheritance."

Sam trotted up to them, his face ecstatic. There was nothing in the world like riding Zara. No excitement was equal to it, and he could imagine nothing that would better it. She moved with precision, and was a joy to ride. He slipped from her back and stroked her neck, and she nuzzled into his shoulder, adoring him.

Richard was conscious of brief jealousy, and he grinned to hide it, chiding himself for absurdity.

"We must do something about your riding, Sam," he said, and Sam led the mare to the stables, his heart racing with pleasure, and as he dried her and groomed her, working until her coat shone and her mane and tail were a silken glisten, he dreamed of racing her, of riding her to win, of the roar of the crowd as he brought her to victory, and of the day when he would lead the jockey tables with the most wins of all, and people would look down the racing page and say, "Ah, Sam Lethwaite's riding today. I'll put my money on him."

It was a dream to cherish, and Richard, glancing in at the stable and seeing how the boy worked and how his eyes shone, guessed at his thoughts and went to his lunch, smiling to himself. It had been a long time since he too had dreamed dreams, but he remembered how it felt.

CHAPTER *six*

Jed Howarth was driving home in a rare state of euphoria, which was shared by his head man, Staines. Behind them was Ginger King, a magnificent chestnut stallion that Jed and Staines between them had been training over the past season. He had come second in his first two races, and today, running at the top of his form, he had come first by two lengths, having given his jockey the ride of his life.

Jed whistled softly to himself as he drove along the darkling lanes. There was a hint of frost in the air and a crispness in the ground, but all might be well by Monday when another of his horses was running at Newcastle. Jed liked to keep at least two race-horses each season, though he did not train for other people. There was never time.

Ginger King was comfortably rugged up and warm and contemplating home. He enjoyed racing, loved running, and loathed to see another beast's tail in front of him. He had immense stamina and a surprising reserve of acceleration which he could be relied on to produce at the right moment, so long as he was not allowed to run too fast at the start of the race. He rocketed forward in a last sprint that carried him clear of

competition. His warm friendly eyes glowed with
triumph as he passed the post, and his ears were
pricked for the instant praise that he knew was his due.
Jed, with a meal inside him and the horse behind him,
apparently little more than slightly tired by his efforts,
could not imagine that life could be finer.

Staines was content too. He sat smoking, planning future races for both Ginger King and Blue Rocket, their
other horse, mentally going over the race again in every
detail. Bob couldn't have ridden better. The jockey
knew Ginger King well and often rode for Jed. And he
loved horses beyond anything else in life.

So did Staines. He wanted nothing more than to go
on caring for them, bringing new foals into the world
each year, supervising the births, cosseting the mares.
He had a way with horses. He had no distractions. He
had been married, long ago now, and Ellen had been
dainty and enchanting. In those days Staines had been
a jockey, and, a month before their baby was due, he
had been riding at the other end of the country. Ellen
had been alone.

She had fallen downstairs in the night, and no one
had found her. He had come home eager and excited,
having won his race, and found her lying in a twisted
heap. She and the child both died, and he never for-
gave himself for having left her alone at night at such a
time. He gave up riding, and he would never, as long as
he lived, marry again. It still hurt to remember Ellen.
He was safer with horses.

He pushed thoughts of his wife away from him. Ginger King was all set for a great season. He was as fit as it
was possible to get a horse, and though the going had
been firm and the ground a mite harder than the King
cared for, there was no sign of jarring. The King liked
good going and Blue Rocket liked it soft and seemed to

revel in flying turf and mud all over him. He was always at his best when the course was mucky.

The headlights revealed high stone walls, bleached against the dark. The grass at the edge of the road was devoid of colour, and the road itself stretched, narrow and winding, through an endless void. Soon they would turn into the lane for home, and the King would be stabled and warm, and there would be the familiar routine for all of them. Only a few weeks and the highlight of the year would begin, the busy time, the best time, when the new foals came nightly and their mischievous ways amused everyone.

There was always excitement at foaling time, and not even the most indifferent of the men failed to be interested in the youngsters, each one unique—one was timid and one was bold, one fled from men and another came eagerly, searching hands and pockets for titbits. Each explored his new world, upsetting buckets, trying to get out of gates, fighting in mock battle and racing with endless energy round the paddocks with the mares watching and chasing too, teaching young limbs how to exercise and strengthen while the men speculated on each foal's future, trying to pick out the winners that would catch the public eye in the years ahead, trying to spot a successor for the great chasers and racers, a horse without parallel. One day, they would breed him.

It was good to end the day with dreams, and pleasant to drive through the empty lanes, conscious of a day well spent and a race well won, the culmination of weeks of training, of walking and trotting, of constant exercise and frequent schooling, and of the last carefully planned week that would get him fit but not stale, ready to run his best. Good old Ginger King. Another three races, another three wins, and he could retire to stud, and he would have earned his status as a winning sire . . . and would sire winners.

The headlights cut a swathe across the road and, as the car rounded the bend, picked out another car, slewed sideways, wing crumpled against the wall. A single headlight blazed against the dark.

Jed swore and stopped the car and jumped out. Staines followed him. Jed had recognized the sports car. It belonged to Stella Proud. He set his lips. Stella was growing worse, and there was no accounting for it. She had been reckless when she was young, but with a craziness of youth that endeared her to others. This last year she had become impossible, drinking far too much and keeping odd company, shocking everybody by her behaviour. He sighed. Poor Richard. He wondered if she was hurt, and went back to get a torch from his Land Rover.

Stella lay across the front seat. Her skirt was rucked up, and her scarlet mouth was an insult to her face. Heavy eye make-up and a slash of rouge on each cheek added to her grotesqueness. She looked up at Jed and giggled. It was a horrible noise.

"Nice Jed," she said. "Bloody car hit bloody wall. Come here, Jed."

She reached up a scarlet-taloned hand and stroked his cheek.

"For God's sake get a blanket out of the Land Rover," Jed said, as Staines came up. He took one look at her and went off again, his face impassive.

"Come on, Stella. You can't stay here."

Jed helped her out of the car and Staines put an arm round her. She pushed away the blanket.

"Don't like clothes." Her hands went to her skirt fastening.

"You'll catch your death of cold," Jed said furiously.

Staines pulled the blanket tight, imprisoning her arms, and half lifted, half pushed her towards the Land

Rover. She fell into the back, pulling him down with her, reaching up to caress his face with her cheek.

"She's a sight more than half-cut," Staines said.

"I'll have to take her home," Jed said. It meant a long detour, and he wanted the King off the road. Too much travelling was not good for horses and the animal had had a long day. Couldn't be helped. He couldn't take Stella to his home. He was not having her near any of his family. He couldn't leave her. There wasn't any choice.

It was a nightmare journey. Stella began to sing, her voice raucous, a bawdy barroom song that no woman should have known. She tried to sit up and thrust off the blanket, but Staines held her firmly. She bit his hand. He restrained a desire to slap her face and sat stoical, astounded by her strength. She struggled against his restraining hands.

Ginger King did not like the noise. He listened uneasily and began to kick the horse-box.

"Blast," Jed said. "He'll hurt himself. Shut her up."

Staines had no option. He took a clean handkerchief from his pocket and tied it over her mouth, shocked by his own action, by the ludicrous situation, and sickened by the sight and sound of her.

Jed drove as fast as he dared. He had to consider the horse-box all the time, and the horse was a sight more important than the damn fool woman. He frowned, all the contentment gone. He wondered if she were going insane. Richard ought to divorce her. It was bad for Sue to have a mother like that, a woman so notorious that all the Dales gossiped about her.

At last the lights of the Proud stud showed, high on the crest of the hill. Jed changed gear and the Land Rover hauled itself and the horse-box up the last lap, the engine straining. He drove into the yard.

Richard had been treating one of the mares for a cough. He heard the Land Rover and, startled, came into the yard. Jed called to him.

"Jed! Whatever are you doing here? How did the King run?"

"He won," Jed said.

"That's wonderful. Come and have a drink to celebrate?"

Jed shook his head.

Staines released the handkerchief that was gagging Stella, and she gave a sudden scream of rage. She twisted free from his grasp, shaking off the horse blanket, and kicked again and again at his legs, her high heels hurting abominably. Richard's face changed, his lips tightening, his eyes suddenly blank. He was holding a bottle of balsam in his hand, having been making an inhalant for the mare. He turned blindly and put it on the window sill beside him. His hand was shaking.

"Stella crashed her car. We brought her home," Jed said. "Couldn't leave her there."

Her breath hung in the air. Yet she did not seem to feel the cold. Sam stared from the corner of the yard, his face white and his breath coming unevenly. He turned and went into Zara's stall, sickened and shaking.

Vence had vanished too, and Richard came towards his wife, taking off his coat, intending to put it round her shoulders.

"Dear Richard," she said, venom in every word. "Afraid-of-scandal-Richard; always-hide-and-pretend-everything's-all-right Richard; don't-let-people-know-you-have-a-wife Richard; just live with your mares, don't you, Richard? Why don't you sleep with them too?" Her voice was rising, and they stood mesmerized. Sue had come out of the house, alarmed by the noise, and was watching, unable to move, unable to believe her eyes, unable to feel anything but hatred. She leaned against the stone wall and bruised her hands against the roughness, not even noticing. Why couldn't her father do something? Why couldn't he stop her mother? Why wouldn't he divorce her . . . if he knew what the girls at school said he wouldn't be so cruel . . . if only her mother would die. . . . Tears flicked down her cheeks, and the wind was icy.

"Stella." Richard spoke sharply, anxious to try and smooth matters over, to get her to bed, to erase the whole scene from their lives, but Stella had drunk too much to be reasonable. She was elated, knowing her power to make them all cringe, aware that they found her outrageous, aware that every word she said was inflaming the situation, and totally unable to stop herself.

She slipped sideways as Richard put the coat over her, flinging it to the ground. She caught sight of Sue standing speechless, tears rolling down her cheeks.

"Your father ought to have been a stallion, my lovely pretty little daughter. Did you know that? To breed little horses. He isn't human . . . not even halfway human. . . ."

Vence had come back with Nan and Sarah.

"Now, you come to bed, lovey. Come with Sarah then and have a nice warm bed and a nice hot-water bottle. There's a good girl. Come on then. Sarah will make you comfy."

It was nursery singsong, the talk used to a tired and naughty child, and for a moment it had an effect. Stella began to walk with them towards the house.

One of the dogs was in the yard. He came towards them and, quite suddenly, backed away, growling.

Stella wrenched herself from Sarah's grip.

"Teach your dogs to growl at me," she yelled. "I'll teach you . . . I'll teach your mare, your bloody blasted mare . . . she won't run in any races. She won't have any foals. . . ."

She was running towards the stall where Zara listened, her ears back, her eyes rolling uneasily. Sam went towards the door, afraid that Stella might damage the mare. His foot caught something and the snake stick fell forward, fell relentlessly into Stella's hands, and she lifted it and swung out at the mare, but the stick missed her.

Zara squealed and reared, hitting her head on the rafters. Sam flung himself forward and the stick descended across his shoulders and again across his back, but he caught it and held it grimly as Jed and Richard ran forward and pulled Stella away.

She ran towards the Land Rover, screaming, and tried to climb inside. Staines, without even thinking, swung his fist and caught her on the chin. She crumpled to the ground, and Sarah put Richard's coat round her, and she and Vence lifted her and walked towards the house. Richard flung the stick into a corner and went to Sam, not knowing whether to comfort the boy or the mare, but Paddy was already with Zara, talking in a soft singsong, and old Adam, roused from sleep, was there too, looking for lotion and dressings for the cut on her head. She was trembling, but not more so than Sam, or Richard, who could scarcely control his chattering teeth. The familiar knifing pain that was a frequent companion, burning his side, flared to unpleasant life.

Jed and Staines stood helpless, not knowing what to do or say.

"Come back with us for the night, Richard," Jed said.

"I've got the mare to see to," Richard said woodenly. He looked across the yard to Sue, who was standing in

the shadows, unable to control her frightened sobs.
"Jed . . . take Sue. . . ."

Staines went to her and put his arm round her. She leaned against him, desperate for comfort, and all the way back to Jed's home she sat between them, tears pouring down her cheeks, shaking with the shock of the scene she had witnessed, and nothing they could do or say would stop her sobbing over and over, "If only she'd die—"

Richard bathed Sam's weals and dressed them with lotion. There was nothing he could say, no apology he could make. Sam had stayed late to help him with the mares, as two of them were coughing. If only he had gone home at the proper time. Sam himself could find nothing to say either, and was aware that old Adam was muttering behind him and that Paddy was keeping up a steady rhythmic swearing to relieve his feelings. The Irishman left Adam working and went to the Vences' cottage and made coffee for them, lacing it with whisky. It was bitter cold and they had all had a hell of an evening. The woman was crazy . . . going out of her mind —there couldn't be any other explanation. And that one was no help.

Inside the house Stella slept, and Sarah sat beside her, not wanting to leave her alone. She had come suddenly to her senses and flung herself on her bed. She clung desperately to Sarah, who alone offered sympathy and comfort. But Sarah could not still the sobs. She did not know what to say or what to do. She sat there, long after night had come to cover the Dale, and worry needled her. When the Prouds were first wed, they had been so happy, and Stella had been gay and daring, yes, but never like this. What had changed her, and why was she growing worse over these past few months, behaving like a woman possessed? The doctor said it was

the drink and maybe it was at that, but there was no
way of stopping her from getting it. You couldn't lock
her up. . . .

Sarah's thoughts went round her head, and Richard's
echoed them. Something would have to be done, but he
didn't know what or who could help. The doctor had
suggested a home for alcoholics, but she was not that
bad . . . or hadn't been. . . .

Paddy, unable to sleep, driving back to the stables at
three in the morning, found Richard lying, exhausted,
asleep in the straw, while the mare watched over him.
The Irishman fetched a blanket and sat down to keep
his own vigil. Poor bloody devil, honest to God, it was
a wicked shame. But there was nothing that any of
them could do to help. He thought of his own wife,
Bridget, asleep in their house in the village, and was
thankful for her understanding and companionship,
and his five daughters.

Outside in the darkness owlcall and foxcall intensified the loneliness, as the bird wheeled eerily above the
stack on silken whispering wings and the beast stole
along the moorland lane, sniffing out his supper. The
moon, full in a star-dazed sky, shone on the bleak moor,
and the wind whined in the trees. Richard moved and
opened his eyes, and Paddy slipped out into the shadows, knowing he would prefer to be alone. He stared
into the night, wondering what kind of God it was that
let men live in such misery.

Richard filled the kettle and made more inhalant,
and sat with the mare, watching her, pushing away
thought. Existence was only tolerable if he lived from
hour to hour, enduring the brief moment and ignoring
the future. Except for the horses, and they had a future,
and their future coloured his dreams.

seven

The peregrine was resting, high on a telegraph pole. He had escaped from a falconer in the South and flown northwards, making with unerring instinct for country that had once been familiar and from which he had been taken when only a few weeks old.

He was hungry, being unused to catching his own food and as yet young and unskilled. His unwinking eyes watched the undergrowth, watched the grass for a lingering movement, hoping for the unwary flash of young rabbit or the quick slink of a large mouse.

Nothing moved. The wind was icy, blowing from the snowy quarter of the sky, threatening to cover the world with a mask that hid many beasts and revealed others cruelly to seeking eyes. Dark clouds packed the horizon, sulphur-glow lurking behind them, so that the moors' folk sniffed uneasily and prepared for siege.

The peregrine turned his head, watching. The Proud stables were below him, and he stared curiously at the horses. Sam was bringing Zara in from the field, and Chris had two of the colts beside him as he rode Tarzan in from the far paddock. Sue was not yet home from school and Richard was uneasy, fearing a blizzard that

might trap her on the long walk home from the bus
stop down in the village. Vence had taken the Land
Rover and gone to find her. It was more likely to get
through than the Morris.

Sam caught sight of a movement. He had been scan-
ning the sky nervously, wondering if he himself would
get home. When snow fell on the moors it came lashed
by the winds of hell, driving relentlessly out of a night-
dark sky, settling in great flakes that swiftly covered land-
mark and telltale and hid the roads. He had seen such
snowfalls twice in his life, but he had never seen a sky
like this.

"Vence has left your mother a note," Richard said, as
he brought in two of the mares and handed one over to
Chris to put in her loose box. "He thought you'd better
stop here tonight. There's a spare bed in the bunk-
house."

Sam grinned, relieved. Snow, in safety, would be an
adventure. He whistled as he went about his work,
fetching water for the horses and bringing the bales for
Chris to open and tease for bedding.

He fetched hay and filled the hay bags. Each mare
knew him, and even the foals greeted him with a small
whinny of pleasure. Chris watched him, envious. Sam
had a manner all his own with horses. And though they
tolerated Chris, he could never evoke the same re-
sponse. He grinned wryly. It was absurd to be jealous
of a little nobody from the village. All the same, he continued to notice how each mare and colt turned its
head to look at the small fair-haired lad who came to
check the hay bags. Sam was thistledown light, built on
finer lines than most, and his tanned skin and bright
dark eyes, always alert with laughter, had endeared him
to Stella, who found him odd jobs to do and tried carefully not to show her vindictiveness when he was about.

He had found it hard to believe the stable gossip, until he had had proof for himself.

He glanced upwards as he went towards the hayrick. The peregrine was still there. The bird was immobile except for its turning inquisitive head. The brown wings brooded, and the handsome speckled breast was dull in the fading light. Darkness was coming fast and early at three in the afternoon. The horses, restless and uneasy, smelling strangeness, alarmed by the approach of snow, stamped in their stalls.

Chris came to find Sam and found him staring intently. He looked up too.

"It's been here all afternoon," Sam said. "Reckon it's hand tame? It don't seem natural, sitting there, watching us all that time."

Richard fetched the binoculars from the house.

"He's wearing jesses," he said at last. "Or the remains of jesses. . . . Vence has a lure somewhere. Let's see if we can bring him down."

Vence often had a falcon in the little hut at the back of the cottage, but his last bird had died of convulsions, a common end for the species, and there had been none to take its place.

Sam ran to find Sarah, who knew where everything was kept, and who gave him the rook feathers, tied to a long cord. She also gave him a hunk of steak. If the bird was hungry he might come to the hand and feed.

Chris swung the lure and almost before he had time to send it on a second circle the bird was down, his talons clinging to the meat. Sarah brought Vence's glove, and Chris lifted him, and the bird gazed at him thoughtfully. The jesses were intact, and Sam fetched a long leather thong, which Chris fastened through the ring. The bird ignored him, tearing at the meat, holding on delicately with one taloned foot and standing erect to swallow and contemplate before each bite.

Chris had handled only a kestrel before. He had kept one at school, abetted by the biology master, who had gathered a small zoo in his department. They had a young badger, orphaned by a road accident, a fox cub, dug out, almost helpless, by the farmer who had shot his mother after she had raided his hen run, and two kestrels, both of which had come to the school with injured wings.

This bird was different. He was enormous, compared to the kestrel, regal and exciting, and his trust was complete. He was too hungry to care. Chris took another piece of meat and moved him from the lure, which he handed to Sam, who was watching avidly, never having handled a falcon in his life. The bird looked up at him, bent to the meat again, and then stood erect, having fed enough, and ruffled his feathers, so that he was fluffed and enlarged to even greater size.

"That means he's happy," Chris said.

It was almost too dark to see. The first flurry of snow came out of a midnight sky, the flakes large and moist, making the bird shake himself. A horse neighed.

"Put the bird away and let's get the jobs done."

Richard's voice was rough with anxiety. Vence should have been home, long ago, with Sue. The last two miles from the village led over the moor, and it was easy enough to lose the road. There had been many travellers snowbound in the past. Beyond the house, on the far side of the road, not a half mile away, was a small plaque commemorating a woman who had died in the great snowstorm of 1896.

Chris took the peregrine to Sarah. She was used to every kind of beast, whether it had fur or feather, and she tethered it to the block in the shed, talking gently. A human voice always soothed an animal or bird. The bird was well trained and made no sign of protest, content to be among people again and to be well fed after days of hunger and semi-starvation. He had found sanctuary. He had no desire to seek further freedom. Finding his own food was a hard and unrewarding work. He had never known liberty and did not like it.

Sarah went to help bring the last horses into the stable. It was impossible to see far, but sound carried, and she was aware of the Braithwaites working frantically against time to bring the sheep home. There were calls and whistles and the noisy bleating of frightened animals as they pushed on in front of the dogs, as anxious to get away from the threat of bad weather as the Braithwaites were to bring them in. All over the hills, men were battling against time and against darkness, seeking to save the sheep from death in the snow.

Richard checked each animal. Every mare was under cover. Every foal stood in its stall. The yearlings were stabled. The two hunters watched curiously, their heads over the half doors.

He went to look at Zara and see that she was safe and unafraid. Some time after Christmas, probably late in January, he would put her to Midnight. In another year there would be a foal. Such a foal. He dreamed of it at night and saw it now, as he stroked the mare, so real that he was startled to realize that it only existed in his imagination.

Meanwhile, Vence had suggested that they race her, perhaps only once or twice over hurdles, perhaps over fences; perhaps they could bring her on to win one of the big races and the chance of a gold cup. There was no doubt whatever that Sam could ride and should have a start in the racing world. He had to begin somewhere. He only needed to be noticed. There would be plenty willing to give him a trial if he made good.

The snow was driving against the stable doors. He shut the doors, worrying about the morning. Snow, so high on the moors, always meant trouble. There would be drifts through which it would be necessary to dig to fetch hay. And the sheep would need hay too, and all the stacks were beyond the stables. It could not grow darker. If only Vence would come. . . . He looked down the lane, seeking headlights, but there was nothing to be seen. Useless to go and look. That might only mean another of the family lost in the snow.

If Sue had left school late . . . if the bus had been stopped by the snow earlier . . . if she had not met Vence and was walking up over the moors . . . He began to feel sick. His grandfather's stick was lying on the hall table, and he looked at it with sudden horror. Suppose that it really *was* a symbol of bad luck . . . suppose it had been made with cursing and witchcraft . . . that could account for many things. For the untimely deaths of so many of his family, for the ill luck that haunted the Prouds and marred their reputation. Stella was now notorious, the talk of town and village alike, her behaviour wilder than ever, drinking too much, seeing too many men, gambling recklessly, betting heavily at the races, driving like a fiend down the moorland lanes so that it was a wonder she did not have another accident.

He set his teeth. Nothing he could say made the slightest difference, and he was not sure now that it would not be better for Sue if there was a divorce. He had grounds enough, yet he also had scruples and did not want the whole sorry mess made more public than need be, and could not bear the thought of the humiliation that Stella would suffer in the hands of the press and the divorce courts. He felt responsible for her.

He had courted her in a haze of adoration, having never seen any woman so exquisite, and now, in spite of the blurring of the years and the faint coarsening due to her style of living, she was the most beautiful woman he knew, and her slim grace and lovely movement never failed to entrance him, just as the mare entranced him. He knew there was nothing for him behind the façade, yet he could not cast her aside.

She had not known the kind of life he lived, had not appreciated that a man who worked with horses must be a dedicated man. She thought that horses meant wealth, meant excitement, meant an entrance to the racing world and travelling the globe to win in India and France and America, and Australia as well. She knew nothing of the unremitting hard work behind the glamour. Not for Richard the nine-to-five office life, the after-dark parties, the fun of flitting from place to place. His work was always on his doorstep, so that he must be ready to deputize if a groom was ill, must be on hand for the foaling mares, must supervise the breeding and mating, ensuring that all went well, must study the form book so that the foals were bred from winners and sired by winners. In the world of the race-horse heredity was paramount, and the notable sires were a constant, getting youngsters that grew true to expectation and ran according to prediction in nine cases out of ten.

Choose a race-horse, find his sire, and bet with a fair amount of safety if bet you must, Vence said. He himself rarely gambled, but Stella bet heavily, trying to tease stable tips out of the men she knew, rarely backing a winner.

Paddy bet also, tempted to blow half his wages on a likely horse, sometimes bringing off the gamble, more often than not regretful. If the horse hadn't fallen at the first fence . . . ah, for sure, honest to God, the jockey wasn't even trying, arrah, the horse was bumped on the straight. . . . His excuses were many and various, but he never lost because the horse was a bad horse or his judgement at fault. His wife disapproved, but there was nothing she could do to change him and she was resigned to his behaviour. Nobody was perfect.

Richard half smiled to himself, thinking of Paddy. The Irishman had been with him for more than ten years, and though he occasionally drank far too much and bet too heavily, he was hardworking, he loved horses, and he was loyal. Richard had heard that Paddy had nearly landed in jail, beating up a man in the Bell who had dared to criticize Stella. Not that he bore her any love, for she frequently used her acid tongue on him, but because she was the boss's wife and Miss Sue's mother, and Paddy idolized Sue.

He came over to Richard now and stood in front of him, frowning. Paddy was lightly built and lean as a greyhound, with a dolorous greyhound face and long aquiline nose and brown eyes that expressed his feelings more often than he realized. He roused Sarah's maternal instincts so that she mothered him along with the rest of her brood. Having no children of her own, she adopted those that came along, and Richard and Sue and Chris, and Sam and Paddy, were all part of her family and treated as such and fed and cosseted. She had a very special place for Sam, who was endearing, always willing to help and eager to go out of his way to run errands for those he honoured with his affection. He often shopped for Sarah on his way home.

"Vence ought to be back, honest to God, he's been gone forever," Paddy said.

Richard nodded and walked for the twentieth time to the gate. Snow was falling steadily now and leaf and bush and tree were heavy with soft flakes. The road and the moor had vanished, only broken by the darkness of hedge and rock as yet uncovered. Nothing had driven up the lane since the snow began.

"If I took Tarzan . . ." Paddy said, hesitant.

"No," Richard said, anxiety sharpening his voice, "they may have stopped for shelter. . . . They may be at Jed Howarth's place. They had to pass it. Vence is weather-wise and he knows these moors . . . with Sue there, he'd not take chances."

He had to reassure himself, had to think of every alternative but one, and he could not bear to consider that. It took very little snow to pile the road so deep that the way was blocked by abandoned vehicles. There were places where the drivers could shelter . . . if they had time. There had been occasions . . .

He checked the bolts on the stable doors. There was already a pile of snow against Midnight's stable. He could hear the restless rustling as the stallion tramped the straw. He did not like weather. His irritable kick came, thunderous. Richard sighed and opened the half door and quietened the beast. He would hurt himself if they were not careful, and he represented a sizable investment.

Like the mare, and there still might be no foal from her next year to quieten his guilt.

Stella had come into the yard. Sam opened the gate for her and beamed up at her, and she smiled back. Richard heaved a sigh of relief. For some reason she had to impress the boy, and she could usually be trusted to be civil when he was near. He hoped that Sam would not leave the yard. He avoided his wife as much as possible. There was little point in prolonging the altercations that always developed nowadays when they were together.

"What on earth are you all staring at?" Stella asked. She was in one of her rare good moods, having won handsomely on a horse the day before. She had had three stable tips and put ten shillings each way on each horse on a treble accumulator, and all had won. One at

100–6. One at 10–1. And the last at 8–1. She had won over £200, and the warm glow of it remained with her.

"Haven't you seen snow before?" She laughed, still excited by the novelty not only of winning but of winning so much. She put her hand to her forehead and shook her head, slightly dazed. Her head hurt. It often hurt, nowadays, but pain was something she refused to acknowledge. She peered out over the darkling moors where the snow was falling ever more thickly. "What does the poet say? Who was it, that ass Wordsworth . . . ?

> 'The shades of night were falling fast,
> As through an Alpine village passed
> A youth, who bore, 'mid snow and ice,
> A banner with the strange device,
>   Excelsior!'

"You see, I can quote poetry too. You all look as if you were expecting someone to come galloping out of the storm yelling 'Excelsior!' "

"Vence went to meet Sue nearly two hours ago," Richard said. "They're not back yet."

Stella said nothing. Richard glanced at her and saw that she too was looking over the gate with dread in her eyes. She was assailed by guilt, by the knowledge that she had never been a good mother to Sue, that she had failed them all. She railed at the child, annoyed at her lack of beauty. And now, perhaps, out there on the moors . . . she was shocked at the violence of her feelings.

"There hasn't been a phone message?" Richard asked, wondering what was in his wife's mind. He would never understand her.

Stella shook her head.

"I think the line's dead," she said. "I tried to make a

call a few minutes ago, and couldn't raise a sound." She stared bleakly over the gate, and shivered. Even through her fur coat the wind was bitterly cold, and snow mantled all of them, lying on clothing and on hair, whitening shoulders, drifting silently, relentlessly, terrifyingly, until the world was alien and unfamiliar and everything was tainted by deadly fear.

Chris and Sam had gone for comfort to Sarah, only to find that Sarah herself was restless and uneasy, walking from fireplace to window, glancing out into the darkness, listening for the familiar engine sound. Life without Jim was unthinkable, dolt though he sometimes was and maddening as maybe. She made tea for the three of them, and fetched scones and tea cakes, and picked up the Siamese, and sat nursing her, with only half an ear on the boys.

Paddy, coming in through the door, which he let slam behind him, stamped the snow off his boots and shook out his coat.

"Honest to God, it's rotten weather," he said. "I hope it doesn't lie till Christmas."

He looked at Sarah and grinned.

"Now don't you worry, sure as heaven Jim's all right. You could throw him off the top of the rigg beyond the stables and he'd roll and bounce. Honest to God, there's no need for long faces. He's safe in some farmhouse or up at Jed's place, and toasting his feet and feeding his belly, while we're all worrying about him here. You see if I'm not right."

Sarah smiled at him, thanking him for his reassurance, and he put an arm round her shoulder and gave her a quick friendly hug.

"Arrah, me darlin', and if you weren't Jim's wife I'd have you meself, beautiful as you are. Be sure that I would." He made much of his Irish brogue. Anxious to distract her, and himself too, for that matter.

Sarah laughed and poured his tea.

"That's enough of your blarney, Paddy O'Hara. And what about Bridget?"

She looked out at the dark lane, but her expression was easier, and Paddy relaxed, not admitting to his own thoughts, which were gloomy in the extreme.

Inside the silent house, Stella too made tea, and Richard paced the study endlessly. To and fro. Backwards and forwards, uselessly, terrified by his own thoughts, by a vision of Sue stumbling through the snow, perhaps never having met Vence at all. If only he had sent him earlier. If only he had sent him to the school instead of to the bus stop. She might have caught an earlier bus. They sometimes sent the children home if snow was forecast. The moorland villages were well experienced.

"Someone will have taken them in," Stella said. She was voicing a hope and did not want to admit her fear. Richard looked up at her and was startled to see that her face mirrored his own anxiety. Turning to the tray, he saw that for once she had gone to immense trouble with the tea, making fingers of toast and sandwiches, and bringing out some exotic fancy biscuits that she must have been keeping for one of her parties. He dropped into a chair and stretched his hands to the fire, longing for the comfort of warmth. He glanced at his wife.

"Yes, of course." The words lacked conviction, and suddenly, motivated by some feeling that she could not define, Stella put her hand briefly on her husband's shoulder, and was astonished, looking down at him, to see how much grey his hair was showing and how lined was his face. It must have been years since she had given him more than a cursory glance. The guilt that had been needling her ever since she realized that Sue might be lost in the snow knifed her. She would never drink again. . . . She would be a better mother, if only Sue came home safely. She was astonished to find how much she cared.

They sat in the quiet room, where logs blazed in the hearth and darkness hid the stark furnishings, in silent companionship, closer to one another than they had been for years. Outside the window the darkness was intense and the soft snow drifted into corner and cranny, isolating them completely from the world.

The only creature that was easy that evening was the peregrine, asleep on his perch, safe in the knowledge that he was once more among men who would feed him and cherish him and protect him, and that the chancy freedom of the moors and the brutal reality of bleak weather was no longer his uncertain heritage.

CHAPTER *eight*

School had ended early, and the buses had been waiting. Snow was already falling on the surrounding
moors. The drivers were uneasy, knowing, by previous
unhappy experience, how quickly the hills became im-
passable, the drifts mounting between the hedges, the
narrow roads blocked, hill and hummock, rigg and slack,
swang and griff, carr and holl hidden under a bland
cover that no wise man dare challenge, lest he find himself buried or, worse, fallen through the snow into
marsh or bog or crevice. The hills were not for man's
defiance. They killed the foolhardy every year.

Sue, sitting at the rear of the bus, looked anxiously
out of the window. It was a long walk home from the
village, and even on a mild winter day, a raw one. The
wind raced across the moors, ice in its teeth, chilling fingers and numbing feet, so that the few ungathered
sheep huddled under rocks and against the high stone
walls that offered little protection to those who walked
the road.

Farther up the hill, where the wind came ever more
fiercely, the walls were gone, and the wide wild spaces
beckoned, frighteningly bleak, field upon field below

her, the bare sparse-grassed moor above her, and her home, tree sheltered, in the far distance. She hated the long trail up the steep road, hated the climb that took her breath away and the wind that needled through her clothes and rushed on bitter-chill wings past her head, mocking her puny human challenge.

Only in summer were the moorlands welcoming, when green enchantment excited the grass, and thin-stemmed star-bright flowers glimmered in pied beauty, and clouds cast their shadows on the ground as the wind whipped them over the sky.

The buses travelled slowly. Snow masked the land and blotted the view so that time and again the drivers stopped the convoy to wipe the clinging mass from the windscreen, where it had clogged the wipers. The journey seemed endless, through an uncanny landscape where familiar shapes were smoothed to unreality, where the green trees had become Christmas-card reminders of another land, another world, of imagery conjured from a sulphur sky.

Headlights swathed the white. The edge of the road had vanished and only the enclosing walls showed that a road had ever been there. The children were unusually silent, awed by the swiftness with which their horizons had changed and shifted, and though some welcomed the snow and the fun of snowballing and building snowmen, of sledding on the slopes, and two boys at the back of the bus, behind Sue, talked eagerly of skiing, the others had long walks to quiet outposts beyond the safety and comfort of houses and streets and street lights, and had known snow before and were nervous of the darkness and the lack of landmarks.

Cars lined the village streets. Parents had come to meet their children, and one after another, muffled figures came to claim their young. Sue hesitated, knowing that Richard would not have had time, that Stella would never have bothered, wondering if perhaps Paddy or Chris had come for her. It was a relief to see the Land Rover, with Vence standing anxiously beside it.

"It's bad up there," he said, nodding into the darkness. "Not sure what we ought to do."

A lorry came down the village street and stopped beyond them. The driver clambered out of his cab and asked Vence the way to Skipton.

Vence jerked his head towards the moorland road.

"What's it like upalong?"

"How far you going?" the lorry driver asked.

"A couple of miles . . . to the big stone house on the top, with the stables," Vence said.

"It's not too bad. You ought to get that far without trouble." The driver borrowed a light for his cigarette, acknowledged the directions that Vence had given him, and drove away, gears whining as he changed down for the hill that led out of the village.

"Let's go home," Sue said. "They'll be worried."

Vence was not sure. The sky was darker than before, the snow was swirling, and the wind that bit his skin was wicked. If they were forced to stop and walk . . .

"Five of us are going up there," a voice said from the darkness. "We ought to be okay in convoy . . . . Have you got blankets if you do get stuck?"

Vence recognized a farmer from beyond the rigg.

He nodded. Nobody but a fool went without taking precautions in such weather. He had rugs with him, and a flask of coffee, and sandwiches, and chocolate. Sarah had sent him out well provided, not thinking that he might be caught by the weather but sure that they would be late. Sue was always starving, school dinners being what Sarah called "nobbut nibbles and stodge."

They set off, following the bright red rear lights of an old Ford truck belonging to the shepherd at One Tree Farm, which was five miles beyond the Proud place. Vence was glad that he did not have to journey so far. He could not remember such wicked weather, and worse hung in the sky, the clouds pendant above the church tower, the air oppressive with deadened silence, sound converted, noises lost or unfamiliar, so that once, when Vence stopped to wipe away the snow, a dog howling at the other side of the wyke sounded muffled and uncanny, a ghost beast summoning the hounds of darkness from the hidden gateways of Hades.

Fear rode beside them. Sue did not dare comment. It was slow driving, and Vence needed all his concentration. He was aware only of the twin red lights comfortingly ahead, and the dark loom of high walls. Thank God for Yorkshiremen who built strong and stark. Soon the walls would end.

The tanker driving towards them from Kendal was on unfamiliar ground. The other road had been blocked, and he had been diverted. Behind him crawling traffic blessed his headlights and his brilliant unwinking rear lights, for once not sorry to be held back. Overtaking would have been mania.

He crept along, watching the faint telltale of the road edge. He was a young man and snow was new to him, at least snow like this that hid everything within seconds and blew through the cab window, which was open to avoid misting of glass that was only partly clear, even though the wind was behind him and not blowing into the face of the vehicle.

He could not see the corner, had no chance of knowing that here the road forked to the right and a ditch guarded the moor edge, while the bend curved down and away. He followed the misleading line that led

straight on, and a moment later his front wheels were
through crisp snow and on mud, sliding into the ditch,
and his cab was canting, so that his trailer twisted and
blocked the road in both directions.

Behind him cars stopped, men ran to help him clam-
ber free and to stand with him, helpless and bewildered. Fast-falling snow was already covering the sta-
tionary vehicles. Soon there would be nothing to show
but hummocks that revealed their rooftops.

"There isn't a building for miles," one man said.

"There's t' Proud place, just over a mile back. Saw
the lights as we came by. It's on t'other road," a lorry
driver said. He was a local man, and he looked uneasily
over his shoulder, not wishing to challenge the moor.
He was driving back to the village after delivering cattle cake to One Tree Farm. He had had a nightmare
trip.

Vence frowned as the convoy stopped. There were
several cars behind him, and four in front. He got out.

"You stay here, lass," he said and stumped off, a dark
shape, a moving shadow in a world of shades etched
against the background of snow.

The group of men and women around the lorry were
in huddled consultation, beating arms against bodies to
defy the cold. The wind scolded around them, whining
in the telegraph wires that were free from snow, shaking
those where the snow clung so that it fell with a soft
thump onto the heads of those below.

"Nowt to be done," one of the men said gloomily.
"Road's blocked, reet enough. Need a crane to fetch
this lot out."

"Be suicide to try to turn back and make t' village,"
the shepherd from One Tree Farm said. "Ah've been
aht in weather like this and it's nowt but madness to
try."

"We might make the Proud place, where I live," Vence said. "There's room enough for a crowd . . . if we can get there."

"We'll freeze oot here," the shepherd said. "My feet are fairly clumpst as 'tis, and 'tis nowt but a feeding storm. There's worse to coom."

They grouped together, the children laughing and chattering, excited by the unusual adventure. Vence went back for Sue and made her turn her collar up against the wind and put his woollen scarf over her head. She protested, but he insisted. Warmth was vital, and he was wearing a thick jersey and donkey jacket with a hood that he could turn up against the wind.

He glanced at his watch by the headlights of one of the cars. Already past seven, hard as it was to believe, and those at home would be worried sick, wondering. The road ahead was lost to sight. The shepherd had a dog with him, safely bedded on straw in the boot of his car. He whistled the beast to him, and the collie came floundering in the snow, plumed tail eager at first, and then drooping, as the dog battled against the clinging wet that soaked his coat and in which he fell, belly deep, at every step. He whimpered, but ploughed on.

"T' dog's old and way-wise," the shepherd said. "It'll mak' slow going, but if we follow him, he'll know where t' road lies. He's done it before, seeking lost sheep, and ah've never known him put foot wrong. Find t' road, Jock, lad."

The collie struggled valiantly, leaping at each step, and the group followed, Sue kept close to Vence, each movement an ordeal. The road lay uphill; the snow was wet and the surface treacherous. She was not wearing boots, and her shoes and legs were soon sodden. She was tired and hungry in spite of the sandwiches, and the darkness beyond them frightened her, even though she had company. Who knew what lurked in the shadows?

Vence watched the dog. One of the men had a torch which shone in front of him, a fan of light piercing the darkness, which, beyond the edge of brilliance, was blacker than before. The snow had ceased briefly, and above them the clouds parted and a glim shone from a maggoty moon that lay, small and thin, on its back. Clouds pockmarked the surface, and the light that glistered faintly was soft and weak.

Sue had no breath for talking. She needed it to fight the wind that wracked them, that rose to screaming fury as they topped the crest following the slowly moving dog, forgetting all goals save that of finding shelter, of shutting away the cold and the brutal force that blustered at their heels, stirring the snow and breathing iciness with every gust.

One step followed another through the darkness. A brief giggle reached her lips and died unheard, as it occurred to her that the dog was path-breaking for all of them and that they were patiently following in the marks he left in the snow as he made unerringly for shelter.

In his master's steps he trod. . . .

Only they were treading in a dog's steps. She wanted to share the thought with Vence but it seemed too difficult to explain and too schoolgirlishly absurd, and she gave up the effort. The moon lent unreality to a phantom scene, and it was unbelievable to think that only that morning she had walked down the road, with every tree sharp and black against the sky, every bush etched clear. Summer was a distant memory, and Christmas not so very far away, and snowfall unusually early. She hoped the horses were safe . . . and the sheep. . . .

Vence's thoughts were tantalizing. He had let Sue eat all the sandwiches, and as he walked his mind conjured visions of a hearth where a fire blazed warm and of a table spread for tea, on which one of Sarah's pasties waited, golden and delectable, for the careless cut of a knife. The cloth was white and laden with scones and cakes and pancakes, and an apple pie, the crust soft as butter and spread with sugar, and there was tea, hot, strong, and supremely satisfying. His mouth watered hungrily. The vision was almost tangible.

They crested the hill. There, on the branch road that led across the moors, was the black hulk of the Proud stud, the windows welcoming, glowing orange, telling of life and warmth.

The shepherd pointed, and the dog, obedient, nosed out the way and led them on, step by slow step, at a maddening crawl. Once one of the lorry drivers, moving forwards and sideways to catch up with the leaders, floundered into a drift, and Vence and the farmer from over the rigg pulled him clear. After that no one moved off the track that the dog was making.

Sue felt sick with cold. The clouds had left the moonslip islanded in dark, glittering icily, and the bleak shimmer of barren wastes was revealed in all its starkness. There was nothing friendly here. An owl, hidden in a stack near the stables, sent out a long eerie ghost-call and was answered by a plangent note from a tree near by. Echo and echo answer sounded and resounded as the birds hooted their hunger. Nothing alive was stirring. Furred and feathered creatures alike lay low, huddled against the cold that seeped into half-starved bones, and hid from the bitter probes that the wind sent into every cranny. Tomorrow there would be small creatures lying stiff on the frozen surface. Tomorrow the owls might feed, but not tonight, and they moaned their plight together.

The house was nearer. One of the Manor Farm dogs barked, and Sue, looking up, saw the crowding trees that sheltered the farmhouse, hiding it from her own home, and was conscious of a surge of excitement that warmed her briefly and left her colder than ever, as she heard her father's voice and his anxious call into the darkness.

Vence hallooed an answer.

"They're safe," Richard yelled, and Stella grabbed her coat and came to join him, and Sarah, hearing the noise, came running with Chris and Sam and Paddy beside her, and both the Braithwaites left their fire to make certain that all was well. Soon they would have to go back to the barns where the sheep were shut for the night, and put hay for the hungry beasts, but they had stopped, briefly, for food and drink and rest. It had been mortal cold. And a long and tedious job, gathering in the outlying ewes and bringing them home for shelter. It was a frequent and familiar winter task, there on the stark uplands, and the barns were built to house them and to house the lambing ewes. It made the all-night vigils less daunting.

Not so much farther. Sue could see the group waiting for them. Richard had switched on the lights in the yard, and was forcing open the gate, under which snow had drifted and frozen. She began to count the people with her. There were ten men, four women, and nine children, as two of the fathers had volunteered to bring home kids for their neighbors. Twenty-three of them. And several complete strangers among them. It was a good job there were the three houses and that they were always stocked with food for months at a time, and had deep freezes for summer produce and any pigs and lambs that they kept for their own use. They had an arrangement with the butcher in the town, who killed and jointed for them.

Richard was startled by the size of the party that followed Vence up the road.

"Road's blocked," Vence said. "A lorry with a trailer came off on the bend."

There was no time to waste. They were cold, hungry, and exhausted. Sarah marshalled them into three groups, handing over some to the Braithwaites and some to Stella. The shepherd and the dog went to the farm with the lorry drivers, and Stella took the four women and their own children and two of the men into the house while the rest of the party went with Sarah and Vence.

There was little time to greet Sue, to give her more than a brief smile and a quick hug. Everyone was wet and shivering and hungry, and while Stella supervised their drying clothes and found spare clothes of hers and Sue's and Richard's, Chris gave them scalding tea and Richard made a vast pan of soup and dug deep into the freezer for steaks, and Stella came back to cook quantities of chips and to feel, for the first time for years, that she was of use and that life was less wearisome than usual. The pain that often needled her head was easier too. She was thankful to be warm and not outside in the windy dark where the gale had renewed itself, its vigour doubled after a brief rest, and snow drove against doors and windows and piled in the yard and the moon was lost in the heavy mass of cloud, and over the keen of the wind and the shake and rattle as it hurled against loose windows came the hollowing call of the starving owls, plainting their hunger to an uncaring world, and then, sudden and frightening, the scream of the peregrine, alarmed by the noise and the windy dark.

Sue heard him and stared, sure she had heard a creature dying in the snow.

"It's only a falcon," Sam said. "He's scared. We found

him this afternoon. Quite tame and wearing jesses."
The scream came again.

"You'd best bring him in and put him in the kitchen," Richard said, and Sam went into the gale and the dark and battled with the door of the shed and found the bird, which came unresisting, glad of company, and stared with insolent eyes at the huddled wayfarers in their odd garments, as he was taken to share warmth and company.

Sue came to look at him and stroked his soft breast. He put his head on one side and stared at her, and then bent to nibble her wrist with a gentle movement of his beak.

Sue smiled at him.

"We'll call him Storm," she said.

As if to emphasize the name the wind rose to a roar and screamed in dervish fury round the corner of the house, and the bird ruffled his feathers and settled himself on the perch which Sam had brought with him, and, at ease and relaxed now that he was not alone, began to preen himself delicately, settling each feather as he worked.

"Come and feed, Sue," Richard said. He put an arm around his daughter's shoulder, and she leaned against him briefly. It was good to be home.

She went back to the warmth in the other room and watched her mother handing out food and laughing with her unexpected guests.

Richard watched Stella too, and as she busied herself with feeding the visitors, he remembered the parties which she loved giving and suddenly wondered if she found life too boring, with nothing in particular to do and no one with whom she found real companionship. It was a strange thought, which had never crossed his mind before. What was there for her out here in the wilds, when he was always busy with the horses?

He listened to the storm beating at the windows and turned his mind to other things. They might be marooned for days on top of the moors, if the snow lasted, but there would be plenty of extra help in the morning to dig the yard clear and bring hay for the sheep and the horses. Though God alone knew how they'd fare over at One Tree Farm, where they were always short-handed and the shepherd was now missing. A good job they were not yet lambing.

Later that night he lay in the dark thinking of the strangers under his roof and the world outside that was now remote and impossible to reach. He could not even let their families know that all was well.

He listened to Stella breathing. She had moved into his room, and it was odd not to be alone. Perhaps . . . but pipe dreams were for children, and he had little hope that she would ever change. He turned over to face the window, made unfamiliar by the strange light from outside. Stella was asleep in the other bed, her hair spread on her pillow, her face relaxed and child-like, as it had looked long ago.

He put out a hand and touched the warm skin, and she turned and murmured and stretched an arm to him and slept again. He lay wakeful, remembering their honeymoon and the first bright days of marriage, looking back over the long years that had drifted painfully by, with an ache that would not be stilled, and a painful consciousness that his eyes were smarting, and that perhaps much of the blame for the wasted years lay with him, and not with her. It was a lonely thought.

CHAPTER *nine*

Nightlong, the snow continued to fall. Morning came with a brilliant sun that glared off the smooth surface. Drifts lay against door and sill, against stable and stack, so that Richard, waking to silence, looked out of the window and saw nothing but the work that lay ahead.

Stella went down to cook vast quantities of bacon and eggs. Sam had slept in the kitchen chair and woken rumpled and yawning, and had cleaned the paper away from beneath the peregrine's perch and soothed the bird and fed him. The drifts did not lie against the back door, and he went outside and whistled at the sight that met him.

The shape and fold of the moors had vanished. A smooth slope led downhill to the Weere, and the stream itself flowed between high banks of snow that hid the limestone steps and grass edges. Gone were the scanty ribs of ground that showed on the far slope; gone were the rocks that revealed the old bed of the dry stream that once fed the Weere and now only ran with water when snow came off the hills. Soon the Weere would run swift and wicked, fed by rills and runnels and falls that sprang from the depths of the hills themselves and foamed white and wild to swell the peaty waters that thrust brown and savage between the banks. There would be water racing along the village street, and the Bell would once more keep anxious watch, and his grandfather's cottage would fill with the brimming stream, and the mud that lay when the flood had gone would stink for weeks as it had three years before, and there had not been half as much snow then.

No use brooding. He found a coal shovel and began to dig, the exercise bringing colour to his cheeks, his eyes brilliant, so that Stella, coming to call him for his breakfast, looked at him and thought how unfair life was that Annie should have a son like this, an unusually handsome son, while she had only little plain Sue . . . . She would have liked a boy. If she had had one, life might have been different. Richard might have been different too. A son to carry on the Proud tradition . . .

She went inside. The kitchen was warm, and she put her hand to her head. A faint dizziness possessed her, not for the first time, and she reached a hand to the back of one of the chairs. Only one man was, as yet, dressed, the quiet soft-spoken man from London who had made a detour to visit his mother in Skipton, on his way back from a conference in Newcastle. He was a slender man, dark-haired, dark-eyed, with beautiful slim-fingered hands that had strength and cunning of their own. She wondered if he was a pianist or violinist.

There was a fog between her and the room, and she could not see, and the dull throb in her head that came more often these days was back again. He looked at her searchingly and went to her and helped her to a chair.

"Are you all right?" he asked anxiously.

Stella nodded.

"I'm . . . yes, thanks. . . ." The words sounded as if

her voice were not her own. That had happened before
too, but she had always thought it was because she had
had too much to drink. But she had had nothing to drink
for two days . . . not a drop. Fear needled its way into
her mind, and she began to tremble.

He sniffed.

"There's a smell of gas—can't you smell it?"

Stella shook her head. "I can't smell anything these
days—"

He walked over to the gas cooker which they used in
summer, and which Stella had put on to help her cook
all the extra food. One of the jets had blown out when
she opened the door. He turned it off and returned to
her.

"You're all right. Here, drink this." His voice was reassuring, and she took the cup that he had given her,
full of sweet hot coffee. The fog cleared, though the
pain remained. She smiled up at him.

"How silly," she said. "I can't think what came over
me."

The words still seemed wrong. It was ridiculous, as
was the pain in her head. She was never ill. She was
proud of her excellent health and a little scornful of
those who were not so fit, feeling that this was their
fault, rather than their misfortune.

She stood up and was annoyed to discover that the
room had a tendency to sway around her. Determined
not to give way to idiotic dizziness, she began to pour
coffee, but her hand shook, and the man from London
took the pot from her.

"I'd rest for a bit," he said. He grinned at her. "I'm a
doctor . . . my name's Tempest. You'll be all right in a
few minutes. I expect the room's too warm after being
outside in the cold."

Sam was watching her anxiously, and, becoming

aware of him, she made an effort and smiled. She was no longer cold, but her knees felt shaky, and she was reluctant to move. She watched as one after another came in and Alan Tempest took over her task and handed out food. Richard had already eaten and was outside clearing the snow. Sam hurried his meal and went to join him.

"It's going to be tough," Richard said.

Tough was not the word. He had never realized how far it was from the yard to the stacks and back to the stables, and a path had to be dug out every inch of the way. The snow lay thick and deep and treacherous, giving way if a man stood on the surface, and in places the drifts piled up to the stable roof. There were the two stallions, ten mares, several yearlings, and the last batch of foals, and Zara to be fed, as well as Tarzan and his own hunter, Nell. God alone knew how the Braithwaites were faring, over on the Manor Farm, with sheep in the barns and forty cows in the shed and eleven calves, and the pigs and chickens and dogs and the bull. He could hear hungry beasts lowing, and Midnight was neighing, answered by a shrill whinny that echoed along the stable block. And Vence would have to dig his way across the lane.

Richard's thoughts were grim. By ten the men had hacked a way to the shed and found tools, and the remainder of the party joined them, even the children finding spades and lending a hand. One boy, unable to find a spare shovel, had armed himself with a bucket and was gouging his own path to Zara's door. She was irritable, kicking the partition, and Sam called out to her to give over, but she ignored him and the yard resounded with the thud of her hoof against the wood. One of the colts began to add his din, and soon all of the horses were kicking impatiently, the thin air making their appetites even more eager than usual.

Later in the morning a helicopter circled the buildings, and Richard, realizing that the men were probably
checking on stranded travellers, called everybody into
the yard to wave at the man seated in the open door of
the contraption as they came low overhead. Nan,
equally busy on the farm, mustered her guests, and
there was an emptiness when the machine turned and
flew away again, leaving them feeling more cut off than
ever.

Stella rested for most of the morning, but at lunch-
time she was well enough to help Sue and Chris with
the cooking, although she was uneasy, conscious that
Alan Tempest was watching her, as if he were pondering. The knowledge that he was a doctor made her
uneasier still. She had dressed hastily in orange trousers
and a vivid purple jersey and had added a scarlet and
yellow scarf, an outfit which brought odd looks from
the women.

Sue turned on the wireless, wondering if there was
any news of a break in the weather, and they were startled, within a few minutes, to hear the announcer saying
that all the farms on the moors appeared to have far
more than their usual complement of occupants and it
was thought that all the stranded travellers had found
haven. Supplies would be dropped to outlying farms
that afternoon.

They were prepared for the helicopter's return but
not for the amount of food that fell from the sky.
Manna from heaven, Sue thought. There was fodder for
the animals, enough, Richard thought, to stock them
for weeks, and sacks containing packets of soup, tins of
meat and vegetables, flour and lard and butter and
cheese, and several tins of sweets, as well as cigarettes.

Richard was mucking out Zara's stall when Alan
Tempest came to look for him. Tempest had not seen
the mare before, and he marvelled at her elegance. Her

coat shone under the electric light, and her eyes glinted
at him. She watched him carefully, never trusting
strangers, but when he moved slowly and allowed her
his hand to sniff, and gentled her and stroked her neck
and patted her, she relaxed and turned to the wall to
tug at her hay bag.

"What a beautiful creature," Alan Tempest said.
"Are you going to race her?"

"I've entered her for a race at Wetherby in a few
weeks' time. Weather permitting," Richard said. "Sam's
riding her."

"He's certainly the right build," Tempest said.

"He's a first-class rider." Richard flung the last of the
soiled straw onto the barrow, and Chris came to wheel
it away. Vence and Richard between them had found
Sam an apt and eager pupil, and his years of watching
the leading jockeys on the race-course had taught him
as much, or more, than either of them knew.

"Has your wife been ill recently?" Tempest asked, as
Richard put a warmer rug over the mare, anxious that
she should not chill. There was heat in the stables, but
the outside air was colder than he had ever known, and
it was necessary to provide thicker bedding and extra
warmth. He could hear movements beyond them as
Vence and Chris and Sam busied themselves in the
same way. It was a good job there were extra hands,
even if unskilled. The women were helping Stella to
unpack the sacks of provisions, and the children were
snowballing behind the stables, in the garden, having
promised not to venture onto the moors, where the
snow might hide gullies that would trap them or holes
that could break a leg. The snow was streaked with
bird marks, and a thin trail showed where a fox had
gone, dragging his brush.

"Stella?" Richard looked up in surprise. "She's never
ill."

Tempest held the rug while Richard fastened the
surcingle. He did not know what to say. He was a
stranger, stranded for a day or so, and he did not like to
interfere, but it seemed to him that for once, interfer-
ence was necessary and justified.

"She isn't well," he said. "I think you ought to take
her to see your doctor."

"What do you know about it?" Richard asked, the
tone of his voice belying the apparent rudeness of his
question.

"I am a doctor . . . is she subject to unpredictable
tempers? Or to unreasonable behaviour?"

Richard sat down on the edge of the manger. Zara
nosed him and leaned her head on his shoulder, delighted to have company. She hated being alone, hated
the long hours in her stable, and was eager to greet any
of the men she knew, and if Sam or Richard lent her
their time, she was ecstatic.

"I suppose so," he said dully. "I . . . she . . ."

He did not want to reveal the life they led to the
quiet man with the probing eyes.

"I thought she was bored," he said.

Tempest needed no telling. He knew at once of the
misery, the background of a story that he had heard before. The trouble was that few people realized that the
search for excitement, the drinking, the restlessness, the
hunger for new experiences, for new faces, for new
men, were symptoms and not merely character defects.

"She shows signs of actual physical trouble . . . something that can be put straight," Tempest said. Richard
needed occupation. He removed the rug again and took
a curry brush and began to groom the mare, working
in circular sweeps, each movement leaving a metallic
gleam behind on her glorious coat. No wonder the an-
cients spoke of golden horses swifter than the wind and
man had almost deified the beasts, Tempest thought,

watching her. She was sheer perfection. If ever he owned a horse, and he longed to own one, he would need a horse like this. Perhaps one of her foals.

He sighed and reproached himself. Every man needed a dream. He could guess at Richard's, and he could guess at Sam's, and, listening to Paddy cursing because there was no racing and even if there were he could not get out to bet, he could guess at Paddy's. And at Vence's too. There was no need to look farther than the stables for Vence's life, and his contentment was more than apparent. One of the old horse men, horse-wise and dedicated. How many were left?

The mare pushed against the brush, turned to watch Richard with her glowing brown eyes, leaned against him, breathing down his neck so that he thrust her off and said, "Move over, you great booby." She pricked her ears, and he began to hiss to her, the soft soothing hissing of the old grooms, once heard the length of England in every stable, in rich man's house and poor man's cottage, and now rarely heard. Tempest listened, fascinated, remembering his own childhood days, knowing his grandfather's stables and the man who tended the hunters and made the same noise. He was a marvel of patience and could do anything with a horse. He once bought a broken-down race-horse, liking the lines of the beast and sorry that it should be left to rot or to go to the knacker, and brought it back to soundness and rode it for years until it died at the age of thirty of a stomach cancer.

"Will you take your wife to see your doctor, as soon as the snow clears?" Tempest asked.

Richard began to shine the mare's coat with a silk cloth that he kept to gloss her when he had finished brushing. He did not want to face the thoughts that were trying to crowd his mind, but they had to be brought into daylight.

"What do you think is wrong?" he asked.

Tempest hesitated. He did not want to say too much. It was not his place, he was a casual visitor, a passer-by, briefly marooned. All the same he wondered if Fate had led him to drive over the moorland road against his better judgement and had brought him here. He was a religious man, with a deep and steadfast faith of his own that he called on when he was operating. He needed his God to guide his hand through the delicate maze of the human brain. He was a brilliant surgeon, but did not believe that the credit lay with him. There was a Power beyond the world, and he invoked it, always.

"Has she ever fallen on her head?" he asked. "Taken a tumble from a horse?"

"Several times," Richard answered. "But there never seemed to be any particular damage."

"Concussion?"

"Once . . . she had to rest for a fortnight."

"Did she complain of headaches afterwards?" Tempest pulled a bucket from under the bench at the side of the stable, turned it up, and sat on it. Richard began to brush tangles from the silken mane and tail.

"She doesn't complain of her health," Richard said slowly. It was something he had only just realized. In all the years of their marriage her health had never troubled her or seemed important to her.

"When did she start to change? She wasn't always so . . . reckless?"

Richard put his arm round the mare's neck and leaned against her. Her solidity was comforting, as was her warmth and the soft clean tang of her. It was years since he had thought back to the early days of their marriage.

He shrugged. "Stella changed so gradually that I didn't notice at all. . . . I thought she was rebelling against her life here, which is dull in the extreme . . . and I spend all my time in the stables. You have no choice, with horses. . . . But she's only been really—impossible—for the last few months."

"When did your wife have concussion?"

"About a year ago—more or less." The import of the questions began to dawn on Richard. "You mean that all this . . . this nonsense is due to that?" He was completely incredulous.

"It could be. Some slight damage to the brain, followed by a gradual build-up of pressure . . . I may be wrong."

"What kind of doctor are you?" Richard asked.

It was a question that Tempest had not wanted asked.

"A brain surgeon," he said.

"An operation?" Richard hated the thought of surgery.

Tempest nodded.

"Would you personally operate if it were necessary?" Richard asked. There was something about Tempest that gave him immense confidence. This was a man he could trust. Perhaps because he understood horses, and any man with an understanding of horses was an unusually perceptive and patient man in Richard's estimation. There was a quality in such a man that other folk lacked.

"If it can be arranged, yes," Tempest said. "Don't take my word for it . . . and don't tell her. And don't blame her either. . . . I think it's her misfortune, and not her fault. . . ."

Richard rugged the mare and followed the surgeon outside. There was a steady insistent drip from the eaves, and the snow on the moors was pockmarked. The Weere was appreciably higher. The fields would be

flooded and, worse, so would the village. It happened
year after year, and there seemed no cure for it, in spite
of the misery it caused.

"I'll go and help indoors," Tempest said. He had to
operate as soon as he got back to his home town, and he
needed to keep his hands in perfect condition. He had
avoided the outside work, and now Richard knew why.

He watched the surgeon cross the yard and enter the
kitchen. His thoughts raced. If Stella was suffering from
some injury her behaviour was easier to bear, easier to
understand, easier to forgive. If he had divorced her
. . . he blamed himself for neglecting her. Perhaps if
he had been more perceptive. . . . The thoughts
milled in his brain. He had been cruelly unfair.

Sam came out of Tarzan's stall, carrying a feed
bucket and whistling.

"Think it'll clear before the race?" he asked.

"Honest to God, it had better," Paddy said. "I've a
clean shirt to put on you and the mare, Sammy boyo,
and I'm keeping it on ice."

"I'd rather you warmed it," Sam said.

Paddy cuffed him gently. Sam slipped in the snow
and fell backwards, the bucket clattering.

Paddy leaned over him anxiously and helped him
up.

"Arrah, honest to God, boyo, don't do that again.
You're the most important person in this stable, bar the
mare of course, and ye'd look very funny riding without
her. If you hurt yourself . . . you'd best take to your
bed and stay there, or you'll be breaking a leg or an
arm and I'll have nobody for that clean shirt. Don't you
think, sorr, Sam ought to take care of himself? The
whole fortune of the Proud stud depends on the little
whippersnapper."

"I think Sam'll have to learn to take care of himself

for us," Richard said, laughing. "You'll cause him to watch every step and make him nervous, Paddy."

"I'll massage him at night, and exercise him in the morning, and he'd better not feed too much or he'll be putting on weight. Be as fat as butter if Sarah goes on feeding him the way she is. I'll have a word wi' her and it's bread and scrape and no fine vittles for you, Sammy boyo. That mare's going to win if it's the last thing she does."

Richard went back to close the stable door. One of the children had been playing with his stick. It lay in the straw, the tiny dark man's head leering up at him, the snake eyes baleful. He moved it again, aware of an unreasoning antipathy, a superstitious dread that he mocked at even though he admitted it. It was crazy. For all that, he was not having the stick in the stable, and he took it and put it in the old garden shed, storage room for all the rubbish, thrusting it out of sight, as if that would change the luck. He could not bring himself to get rid of it. It had been with the family for too long. It was part of their history. And that too was an unnerving thought. A history of . . . what? Of violent death and human misery.

He slammed the shed door and went in to tea, and found the children playing Monopoly and Stella talking to Tempest, her face animated, her language remarkably vivid, so that for a moment everyone was shocked, and then the other women were laughing as the surgeon described how he had once bet on a race meeting and had a winner in the first race and a winner in the third and had waited for the fifth as the bet on the first two horses was totalled onto the last race. He had heard his horse had won and gone to collect only to find that it had been disqualified.

"Oh well," he'd said philosophically, "I don't suppose I lose much."

"Only eight hundred pounds," the bookmaker had said. Tempest laughed uproariously. "And that's the nearest I've been to winning at the races. Horses . . ."

"Don't talk to Richard about horses," Stella said. "Once he starts, he'll never stop."

Richard picked up his tea-cup and a slice of cake, and stood by the window, watching. He felt curiously remote, his mind half filled with thoughts of his wife and half with thoughts of the mare. He glanced at Sam, who was taking a second slice of cake and who, seeing Richard's eye on him, hastily put it back and blushed. He needed to make sure his weight was down or he would have to waste before the races, and he was not sure that he could do that. At seventeen, his appetite was hearty, and though small, he had to fight a tendency to stockiness.

Outside the window the steady drip of melting snow was more insistent. Day was drifting into dusk, and a twilit owl flew silently across to the barn and perched on the roof, eyes seeking hungrily over the ground.

Richard went into the kitchen and found the peregrine on his perch, also watching the darkness beyond the window. He stroked the bird's soft breast and was rewarded with a friendly nibble. Storm had found sanctuary and was grateful for it. And for once, Stella had not protested.

CHAPTER *ten*

The next two days had, in retrospect, the quality of a dream. The thaw was temporary. More snow fell, and hours were spent digging out the hay, making paths to the beasts, feeding and cleaning them. Everything was difficult, and had it not been for the extra help from the unexpected guests, they would never have managed.

Richard was pleased to see that Stella seemed better, showing no desire to drink too much and less peculiarity in her manner. Sue was more animated than she had been for weeks, laughing and joking with the children, thoroughly enjoying a break from school, and sledding on the slope when there was time to spare. The shouting children gave an air of holiday to everything, and with enough food to last, nobody was too anxious.

By the third day the telephone was repaired, and the marooned travellers sent messages to their relatives, friends promising to inform any who were not able to be reached in such a way. Richard stopped briefly for coffee, which Alan Tempest had made as he was not engaged in manual work. Stella was unusually quiet, and her husband glanced at her uneasily.

Tempest stepped outside the back door and looked at the spill of the fells, covered in deceptive even white-

ness, sloping steeply to the river. The thaw had begun
once more, and there were pockmarks where the surface
snow had melted. The yard was alive with people, and
the horses stood with eager heads over the half doors,
watching the activity with interest. Ears pricked forwards to catch voices, and the children often stopped to
pet one or the other and offer sugar lumps. Richard
could not forbid them, although he disapproved, but
he did ration them, and when the smaller children
wanted more, substituted half carrots and half apples
which were accepted with immense pleasure.

Richard joined Tempest and looked thoughtfully
over the fields. There would be no chance of reasonable
exercise for the horses for some days, and his guess was
that the thaw would be followed by a freeze. It was
going to be difficult to have Zara fit. She would become
slack and lazy, cooped up in her stable, and he did not
want to give her too much work too soon. The weather
was a curse.

"My wife is very quiet," he said, glancing over his
shoulder at Stella, who was turning over the pages of a
magazine. She had spoken little that morning and
seemed remote from them all, removed to some realm
of her own in which they could not share.

"She was very excited when I came downstairs,"
Tempest said. "I gave her a sedative. I had my medical
bag with me. One never leaves such things in the car.
I'll leave some for you, and a prescription. You'll need
to keep her well doped or you'll have more difficulties."

Richard frowned.

"I wish we could get her to our doctor. . . . Is this
trouble likely to get suddenly worse?"

Tempest shook his head.

"Not dramatically suddenly. But it would be as well
to fix things up as soon as possible. I'm pretty sure she

has a meningeal tumour in the frontal lobe area. . . . It won't be malignant, that I can almost guarantee."

"Almost?" Richard said wryly.

"One can never be specific. And I could be wrong. But if it's that, it's curable. She'll be much more subdued after the operation, and you'll find her completely changed, quieter than you have ever known her. But all these distressing behaviour symptoms will vanish. They're due to pressure."

"When the snow goes . . ." Richard said. "I can't force her to go to the doctor . . . and she goes off for days at a time."

"I suggest you immobilize the cars. She won't want to walk over the moors. And get your doctor to come up here. I should tell all your men so that they always take the rotor arm out of the vehicles and keep it safely on them. She mustn't drive when she's liable to these attacks of loss of vision. Also she may get into trouble for drunken driving. . . . You don't want a court case." Tempest lit a cigarette and looked out at the stables. The weather was warmer, and there was a steady persistent drip from the eaves. Snow slithered suddenly off the roof above Zara, and she kicked out with her hind hooves, startled, while the mare in the next loose box whinnied in alarm.

The stable cat was introducing her kittens to the snow. They rolled, fighting and biting, jumped, front paws together, small noses whitened, and one of them, more timid than the rest, tested each step with a hesitant paw, plainly hating the cold. The dogs from the farm and from the Vences' cottage were romping with the children.

"I'll write your doctor a note," Tempest said. "And also watch your wife if she does any cooking. She's lost her sense of smell, and when the gas blew out yesterday she didn't even notice. Luckily I was there."

"Will it come back?" Richard asked. This could be a tremendous disadvantage. He would have to have all the gas removed and make the house all-electric.

"I hope so. Don't worry." Alan Tempest smiled at Richard.

He went inside to talk to Stella, and Richard went over to the stables. He found Vence and sent him for Paddy and Chris and Sam and, while the man was gone, took the rotor arms out of the Morris and out of Stella's sports car, which he had collected the previous week from the garage, repaired after her accident.

The arrival of the snow-plough brought fresh interest to a situation that was becoming tedious. Everyone was anxious to get home, to start life again where it had left off, begrudging the time spent out of touch with families. The children were bored, no longer enchanted by the novelty, and Richard had forbidden playing on the slope as the snow began to melt, afraid that the runners of the improvised sleds might cut into the grass and ruin whatever was left of the grazing. It was astonishing how many trails nine healthy children could make in the snow.

The falcon had become part of the family, alertly intrigued by people. Richard wondered where he had been in the years since he was fledged. This was no wild bird, but a bird used to handling and to busy comings and goings and quite unperturbed by them. Even Stella tolerated him. The sedative made her much easier to live with, and she did not attempt to protest when the children brought the kittens into the kitchen and played with them on the rug by the fire. One of the kittens crawled towards her, and she put down a finger, amused. Nor did she grumble at the untidiness in the house, which no one had time to remedy. It took all their time to prepare meals for so many and to clear up afterwards. She was so remote and quiet that it was uncanny. Richard was aware of her, sitting by the fire, unnaturally inert and inactive due to the sedative.

By midafternoon the snow-plough had returned with the news that the road was free as far as One Tree Farm and that anyone with cars on this side of the blockage could now get home, so that most of the visitors left, and the stables and farmhouse were quiet again.

It took some hours for the breakdown gang to shift the lorry and trailer, and when they too were gone Richard drove Alan Tempest and Vence to collect their vehicles, and Vence went on to the doctor with Alan's note, while Richard drove home again. Sarah had gone to sit with Stella and had promised to tell Sue about her mother's illness.

Richard found Sue waiting for him a mile along the road from the farm. She had Nan's new young guard dog with her, a handsome Doberman called Brutus. He was ten months old and lollopy with youth and high spirits, delving in the remaining snow with eager paws that sent flurries over everyone, apparently enjoying the remonstrances that he brought on himself, full of high good humour. He answered at once to any command, and Sue was entertained by his antics.

Richard slowed the car and stopped, and at once Brutus jumped into the back seat, where he sat regally, looking out of the window. He loved driving. Sue climbed in beside her father.

"Sarah told me," she said.

Richard did not know what to answer.

"Daddy . . . if only we'd known. . . . Sarah says it's quite a commonplace operation and Mummy will be okay afterwards . . . and better. When do you think she'll go into hospital?"

"We have to wait for the doctor to see her," Richard

said. "Dr. Tempest says there's no need at all to worry, and he also says he'll do the operation himself."

"I liked him," Sue said. "It's awfully quiet now everybody's gone," she added wistfully. "All Sam and Chris can think of is whether Zara will be able to race. . . . Sam wants to be the best jockey that ever rode. He says this is his chance."

"We'll just have to wait and see," Richard said. It was all you could do in most situations in life. He was used to the fact, but Sue was impatient and hated uncertainty.

Richard sighed. He wanted to race the mare and have her win at least twice before he put her to the stallion, but time was getting short and he wanted to breed from her soon. He had until March. He wanted the foal born at about the end of the following February. Otherwise it would be at a disadvantage.

He frowned, thinking over the racing rule that states that the age of a horse is reckoned at the beginning of the year he is foaled. This mean that any foal born in December would be technically one year old on January 1, so that when he entered for races he would run with the three-year-olds but be a year younger and at a tremendous disadvantage, which would stay with him all his life. No race-horse should be born until the beginning of the year, which gave him the advantage of ten months when competing with others. Zara would be in her fifth year come January.

If they did not race her in the next fortnight there were three other chances. He did not want to take her any distance. The mare was not used to travelling, and he had neither the time nor the inclination to go far away from home, especially now. Stella's illness complicated matters. Yet the stud was part of their livelihood and beginning to pay its way.

"I must get Vence to make sure Zara is used to the horse-box," he said. "He'd better take her for a short drive every day, round the lanes. Otherwise when she starts racing she may be upset by travelling."

Sue looked at her father in astonishment.

"Don't you care about mother?" she asked. "Will you race Zara even if she's in hospital?"

"I don't know," Richard said unhappily. "It depends on so many things."

Sue jumped out of the car as they drew into the yard and whistled to Brutus. She took him back to the farm without a glance at her father.

Richard sat still. It was too hard to explain, to tell the child that horses were his living, his way of life, his necessity and that while he was steeped in anxiety for them he could chase away the panic that dominated him whenever he thought of his wife. Operations entailed risk, and a brain operation the worst risk of all, and overriding everything else was the urgent overwhelming thought that he could not communicate to anyone, that he had been negligent and lacked understanding, had believed only what he wished to believe, and had he been less involved with the horses and more aware of his wife and her needs, he might have realized what was wrong.

The sense of guilt flared to knifing uneasiness, making his head ache. He wished he could punish himself for his stupidity, wished he could make amends, wished he could show Stella how he felt. He climbed slowly out of the car and removed the rotor arm, and stood, staring down at it, as if it could answer his questions.

He sighed, and sighed again, aware that now he would always blame himself for negligence and that if Stella died. . . . The thought had not been allowed form before, and he stopped on his way to Zara's loose box and stared at the last dregs of snow, and the sudden desperation that assailed him came straight from the depths of hell, of an intimate personal hell that no other human being could share.

Paddy, coming out of the stables with a bucket which he had just scoured under the tap, saw Richard and stopped, shocked by the man's stricken face.

He put out a hand and touched Richard's arm, a gesture that was entirely alien to him.

"Honest to God," he said. "It will be all right, it will be all right, sorr. And I'll pray for her and ask the priest to pray, and it will be all right."

Richard looked at him sombrely.

"Thank you, Paddy," he said, and added on impulse, "if only I'd understood."

"Anyone can be wise by hindsight," Paddy said. "It's having the foresight to look behind ye when you don't know what is in front that is the trouble."

Paddy was rarely so Irish, and Richard was forced to smile. It was kindly meant even if the sentiment was so involved that he could not for the moment work it out.

"Where is my wife?" he asked.

"She went to lie down and rest, and Sarah is in the house," Paddy answered. "Sarah says to tell ye she will sleep in the house if ye like . . . she thinks it might be better. And if ye need anything at all out of the way or any of us can do anything . . . we're all sorry, honest to God," Paddy said, becoming more and more involved and embarrassed as he tried to express himself.

Richard walked into the stable, and Paddy followed him, dumping the bucket beside the door. The two men stood in companionable silence, watching the mare. She was solace and comfort. She was absolute perfection and beauty. She was splendour embodied.

A shadow crossed the door. Stella stood there, looking in at them. Richard glanced at her fearfully, but she smiled up at him.

"Dr. Grey has just come. . . . He's told me, and he wants to see you. Richard?"

She put out her hand blindly. Fear had settled on her, pall-like. Fear of the future and of things unknown. Fear of what might happen to her, what might be happening even now. The sedative that Alan Tempest had left for her blunted the edge of terror but did not take away the nagging undercurrent of worry.

Richard took her hand, but she moved away from him and went over to the mare.

"Whatever happens, you must race and breed from her," Stella said. "We ought to call her foal Proud Hope . . . the Luck of the Prouds. . . ."

Paddy picked up the cloth that glossed the mare's coat and began to rub her. She leaned against him sensuously. She loved the feeling of hands working on her and revelled in her grooming time. Paddy began to whistle under his breath. The work was all to pot, and nothing done at the proper time, but if the snow went perhaps they could get to rights again. The soft hissing went on. Richard followed Stella towards the house.

A few minutes later Adam put his head inside the door.

"How's Zara?" he asked.

Paddy grunted. The mare dipped her head to him and suddenly, without any warning, went over on the straw and rolled. Paddy jumped clear and stared at her. He called to Adam, who helped him ease Zara onto her feet. She leaned her head on Paddy, her eyes staring at her side, and began to paw the ground.

"Colic," Paddy said. "And honest to God, please God it's nothing worse."

"Having fodder at all hours and all at sixes and sevens . . . everything hapsha rapsha," Adam growled.

"Get Vet over. Can't take chances wi' this one . . . and no use bothering Mr. Proud. He's enough to carry on wi'."

The mare was rolling again, her legs driving at the air.

Paddy ran to the telephone while Sam and Adam brought her to her feet, anxious at all costs to stop her lying down. The yard was still covered in a film of snow and frozen on top, and she could not be taken outside.

"Walk her up and down the passages, or take her through to the back of the stables and into the big barn. It's only a step and it's empty," Paddy said, coming back to talk to Sam. "Rug her up first." He had removed the rug to groom her.

He watched them leave the stable and reach the barn safely. Movement eased the mare. He stood in the doorway, cursing.

"Honest to God, there's no end to the ill luck," he said.

This time it was Adam who grunted.

CHAPTER eleven

When Paddy came into the barn some minutes later, Sam was walking the mare to and fro. Her eyes were uneasy, and every time Sam stopped, her head went down and she glared at her belly, as if trying to find out what it could be that made her so uncomfortable. Once she rolled over and thrashed at the air, groaning. Her eyes were puzzled. She could not understand the sudden violent pain that knifed her.

"Is she very bad?" Sam asked. He could not bear to see her suffering.

"Vet's on his way."

Paddy walked over to the mare and looked at her carefully. She had not been fed at the proper times because of the snow, and had been so hungry that she had bolted her feed. In which case this might only be a mild attack of colic . . . and what was more, most probably some of the other horses would suffer too. They were going to be busy. And Mr. Proud was also going to be busy, trying to get his wife into hospital. She would go to Manchester or London, as Alan Tempest was to operate. Nothing but problems.

Vence came into the barn, his face anxious.

"Never rains but it pours," he said irritably.

"Though not surprising if they do get colic after the last few days. Never got one of them fed in reasonable time with the snow to contend wi', and she's not on her normal diet either. Did as best we could. . . ."

"You take over," Paddy said. "We can try a drench. Is there any ready?"

"Don't like keeping it made up," Vence said. He had once read of a horse that had died because medicine had been put in the wrong bottle by a stable lad, who wanted the usual bottle for some ploy of his own. The new bottle had not been cleaned out and had once contained poison. You never could be too careful.

Paddy went to the medicine cabinet and mixed medicinal turpentine with linseed oil and added whisky and ground ginger, making the mixture that Richard favoured as being least likely to do harm whatever the kind of colic. It was also soothing. Zara, when Paddy returned to the barn, was stretched on the straw, sighing heavily.

"I think it's only the result of too little exercise, irregular food, and cold water," Vence said. "She seems easier already."

"One of the colts is showing signs of the same trouble," Chris said, coming in a moment later. "Adam's with him, and I've just given him some of the drench to give the colt. He says that's what's wanted, and it's through being cooped up and having to wait till they were too hungry. They all gobbled and got indigestion."

"Adam's usually right," Vence said, glad to have his opinion confirmed. He watched the mare regain her feet. She was uneasy, quite unable to comprehend why pain had gripped her. She rubbed her head against Sam's shirt, seeking comfort from contact. Sam held her head, and she stood calmly, as if knowing that they

meant to help her, and Paddy brought a warmer rug
and put it over a layer of straw on top of which was a
jute rug, to stop the blanket becoming soaked in sweat.
She was perspiring freely.

"Keep her walking very slowly," Vence said. He was
listening for the vet's car and aware that the doctor's
car was still outside in the yard and that there was no
sign of Richard. If the mare had something worse than
colic . . . she could have a twisted gut . . . she could
have so much gas inside her that her diaphragm might
rupture and she'd die of suffocation . . . the most valuable beast in the stables, their beautiful mare . . .

Sam, watching her, saw his dreams wither and vanish
. . . saw the races that she would win disappear faster
than the melting snow. Saw her lying stretched and
stiff, dead because they had been unable to attend to
her properly, dead because of the snow that covered the
countryside, dead with the other beasts that were buried or frozen or suffering from cold and from exhaus-
tion. There would be other horses, but he did not want
to ride them. He wanted Zara beneath him, flying to
the finish, speeding as only she could speed. He would
never become famous without her to boost him into the
public eye. She was part of his future, his luck, his mas-
cot. The first horse he had ever known really well. He
had mastered, but never made friends with, Jed's magnificent stallion, and their association was a tacit truce.
Zara and he were an entity, needing each other to be
complete.

The vet, coming in through the doorway, made him
jump. Rob Dunset was part of the stables, as familiar to
the horses as Richard and Paddy and Sam and Vence.
He spent more than his working time with both Richard
and Jed, and was one of the rare vets in the country who
knew horses well. He rode them, and he competed in

both show jumping and steeple chasing, and he usually
kept a horse in Jed's stable, which Jed trained for him,
as a favour. He bet more than he could afford, but never
having found time to marry, and living with his mother,
who devoted herself to her son and to his work, he found
no need for money for other than basic necessities, and
he took little heed of either wins or losses. He knew
horses well, and more often won than lost, but when he
bet he bet heavily.

He looked at Zara now and examined her carefully.
She trusted him implicitly. The drench that Paddy had
given her was already easing her, so that she stood quietly. Her sighs were fewer.

"It's only a mild attack," Rob said at last. "Not surprising after the last few days. You'll probably find some
of the other horses affected too. Don't walk her too
much, Sam, or you'll tire her. I'd put her back in her
stall soon and stay with her and watch her. I don't
think she'll get worse."

He went outside and walked through to look at the
other beasts, noting that in spite of the snow the work
was done and well done and each loose box was spread
in clean straw, and Adam was working on the frozen
pipes, trying to thaw them without damage.

"Makes for hard work," Rob commented to Sarah
Vence, who had come over with hot coffee for the men
and who handed him a cup, which he took gratefully.
There was an icy wind cutting across the slope and stirring the trees, which moved with a thin icy brittle
noise, quivering in the hazy sun that lightened a pallid
sky, faintly blue as a fading day.

Vence came to join him. "Will she be well enough to
race?"

"I think so. It's only a mild attack," the vet said,
looking thoughtfully at the row of interested equine

heads that watched him over the half door. He went to talk to Midnight, one of his favourites, and the stallion welcomed him with pleasure. Rob had a way with beasts, and often a frightened dog or terrified cat relaxed when he handled them, half hypnotized by his gentle voice and soothing hands and the eyes that looked deep into the fear-full beast eyes and reassured them. Anger drove him to excessive ill temper and outspokenness if he found an animal in pain through man's neglect. He had no patience with people who took on the responsibility of a pet about the house and refused to care for it to the best of their ability.

"I hope we can get her fit," Vence said. "Wonder if we'll ever get the place right for exercise. It's early in the year for bad weather . . . and looks as if there may be more to come, judging by the sky."

Rob looked across the moors, still patched by snow, here and there the ground showing black against the trampled surface, crossed by sled lines that the children had made and their frequent footsteps, the unmarred expanse having provided them with challenge so that trails crossed and criss-crossed the fields. On the horizon sullen clouds built up to bulk large and the sky glowered.

"I'd best get off," Rob said. "Can't do with being snowed up here. I've got a house full of sick animals, as I couldn't get to their homes, and they've been brought in to me. One little bitch that was in trouble whelping came in on a sled on Monday, wrapped up in a blanket, lying in a basket strapped to the runners. One thing, the odd mode of travel seemed to distract her from her pain, and we soon had her comfortable. Four nice pups."

Richard came out of the house, his face sombre. The
doctor walked beside him. Seeing Rob, they turned to-

wards him, and Richard's face became even more anxious.

"Is something wrong?"

He looked accusingly at Paddy and Vence.

"You should have fetched me."

"Zara has colic . . . she isn't bad." Rob was instantly reassuring. "She'll be quite all right tomorrow. Just a matter of unusual feeding hours. . . . The weather has a lot to answer for, one way and another."

The doctor nodded.

"I've had two old ladies die of exposure in their own cottages this weekend," he said. "No central heating and sleeping in bitter cold rooms . . . and not enough money for fuel for body or home. . . . It's a cruel enough world."

"There are searchers out for two children lost in the snow beyond Lancaster," Rob said. "We never get used to it in this country . . . don't teach the kids to be way-wise, and travellers take insane risks. Yet our mild climate is a myth. Ask any shepherd who has to spend his time on the fells or the moors, or even on the Sussex Downs, what kind of winters we have. He'll soon tell you." He nodded towards the sky. The clouds were nearer, and a sombre glow shone from the brooding mass.

"And there's more to come."

"I'd best be away," the doctor said. "I'll make arrangements, Richard . . . and don't worry. An X ray first . . . but I'm pretty certain Tempest's right. . . ."

Richard, his face bleak, watched him drive away. He roused himself to speak to Rob, who knew him well and who asked directly if Sue or Stella were ill.

"They think Stella has a brain tumour," Richard said.

Rob, startled, looked up at him, and then, as he rapidly reviewed the past months, the picture slipped into focus, and he said to himself, "I might have guessed. . . ."

He had known Richard all his life, and he had known Stella since his friend married her. He remembered her when she first came to live in the house on the fells . . . young, gay, amusing, with the reckless streak in her that sent her to the front when they went across the Pennines to Cheshire and rode to hounds, that sent her car speeding ahead to win in the rallies she used to drive in, that made her the centre of attention in any room she graced. Her beauty had attracted many, but she had little time for any of them. She had loved dancing and amusing herself, sought gaiety and popularity, only because she was a spoiled and beloved daughter, and she and her sister had never lacked for anything. Most of her wilfulness was due to that and her genuine inability to understand the finances of the stud that Richard ran. There was no malice or wickedness in her. Only thoughtlessness and frivolity.

She had only changed for the worse during the last year. Everything pointed the same way. Tumours in animals meant odd behaviour and excitement and unpredictability. In humans every carefully guarded inhibition vanished. . . . He should have guessed. But it was easy to be wise by hindsight.

"You mean you knew?" Richard asked.

Rob shook his head.

"I should have guessed, though," he said. "It all adds up. She just isn't responsible."

"I can't forgive myself," Richard said.

It was the nearest to confession that he would ever make, and Rob, driving home over the icy treacherous roads, was haunted by the desperation in Richard's voice and the blind despair that, for a moment, shadowed his face.

Left alone, Richard went to the mare, who was standing in her stable. Sam had dried her and renewed the straw on her back and put the jute rug back beneath her blanket. She gazed at Richard, her handsome head framed in wisps of straw, and he went to stroke her.

If she died, it would be fair justice, he thought bleakly, a suitable punishment for his obsession with the horses. He could not forget his guilt, and he was not in the habit of justifying himself. Yet no one else in the world would blame him, not even his wife, once she was recovered.

He did not hear Sue speak to him. She went away, upset by his inattention, to find Chris and gain comfort from his company. Nobody seemed to have time for her, and her father's neglect hurt her bitterly. The world, at seventeen, was too sharp-cut, its hues all black or white, and nothing in between, so that she did not see that for her parents there was an area that was not so well divided, where good and bad overlapped indeterminately and reality could be so cruel that it distorted relationships, and left little time for the consideration of others. She would learn, in time, but now she only saw her parents' apparent indifference to her, not knowing that Richard was enduring a private hell that she could never share or that her mother, her mind blurred by pain and drugs, her personality twisted out of recognition, now lived in a shadowed world of unreality, where imagination had taken over and fear gained hold. Only Sarah, completely sane and down to earth, motherly and comforting, could penetrate the drifting twilight and bring her mother reassurance. Neither Sue, nor Richard, for the most part, existed for Stella. And pain, recurring, grew steadily worse.

CHAPTER twelve

During the weeks that followed, everybody relied on Sarah. Sarah, motherly and comfortable, with a fresh outlet for the thwarted maternal feelings that dominated her, found time to talk to Sue, to try and comfort Richard, to devote herself to Stella, who increasingly often found herself unable to see properly, and who, although constantly under sedation, nevertheless found cause for fear.

She clung to Sarah, needing her desperately, using her as a substitute for her own mother, who had died some years before. Sarah's common sense was reassuring. Her brusqueness hid immense kindness. She took over all the household tasks and prepared meals for everyone, feeding them in the house instead of in her cottage. The kitchen in the stone house became as comfortable as that in her own home. She brought in her wicker armchair and the big fireside rug, and the animals followed her, accepting that her presence gave them a right to come too.

The promised snow fell but did not lie. Heavy rain cleared away the last traces, and life began to take on a more normal aspect. Richard drove Stella to the hospital in Bradford for her X ray, and two days later the

doctor called to tell them that they should make arrangements for an operation as soon as possible. Richard
would take his wife to London and stay in a hotel close
by.

"Zara's still entered for the race at Wetherby. It's just
six weeks from now," Vence said before they left. "Shall
I withdraw her?"

"Let her run." Richard was definite. Vence and
Paddy could look after the mare as well as he. Sam
would be too disappointed if they withdrew. And he
had promised the lad, and she was already in training.
"You and Paddy and Chris can go over, and take
Sue with you—it'll distract her, poor kid. Sarah too if
she wants."

It was easier to travel to London by train. Vence
drove them to the station, and Sue watched from the
gate, frightened by her father's irritability when anyone
spoke to him and by her mother's complete withdrawal.
She seemed unable to talk to anyone and looked at Sue
blankly when she said good-bye. It was so strange to see
her quiet. She had always been so noisy and restless,
filled with impatience.

"She's not herself, love," Sarah said, but there was
small comfort there. When had she ever been? The past
years had been bitter, and Sue was only anxious for her
father. She could not believe that all her mother's troubles were due to a lump inside her head. They were
just saying that, glossing things over, the way grownups
did. Making excuses all the time.

Zara had recovered, and Vence had taken over Richard's training programme. He looked at the schedule
now. She was in fine condition and beginning to muscle
up. Sam had taken her out for a brief canter and a short
schooling over fences. And tomorrow he must see that
she had a half-speed gallop. The ground was a shade soft,

but they could see how she went. Three of the three-year-olds were training with her, and Paddy and Chris and he would ride against Sam, so that the mare became used to running in company. She hated to see a horse pass her. The trouble would be to hold her back and prevent her from making too much effort too soon. If she did she might not have the strength to stay the course. There was a lot to learn, and Sam was as green as Zara. Six weeks to go.

By then Stella would have had her operation and should be well on the road to recovery. By then, with luck, the mare should be fit to run—to outrun every beast in the race. She could have done with an extra two weeks' training, but the snow had robbed them of time. Richard and Vence had studied the entry carefully. There were only three horses to fear. One of those had two wins to her credit; one had come second three times, each time being beaten by a well-known animal. The third had a record of wins, but had been pulled up in her last three races. Vence thought she had leg trouble.

Five weeks to go. Get her fit, keep her fit, make sure she was not bored or stale. And it all depended on him. Richard phoned every night, but he was distracted. And Sam was most surprisingly suffering from nerves, sure he would fail them, brooding over Zara, hypersensitive to every movement.

Was she limping? Was that a lump near her knee? Was she blowing? She sneezed, her nostrils full of chaff which she had unwisely sniffed, and Sam wanted to get the vet at once.

"For heaven's sake, lad," Vence said, exasperated. "You're worse'n a lass wi' her first bairn."

There was so much to do, and so little time. Sam studied the training schedule, poring over it. Feeds four times a day. That ought to have been easy, but the mare, since her colic, had suddenly become choosy, picking at her food.

The donkey was brought in beside her. He ate voraciously, and sometimes she fed quietly beside him. At others, she refused altogether. Adam took over her diet. He was always good with faddy beasts. He tempted her with chopped carrots, with fresh greens, when he could find them; changed from oats to horse cubes and back to oats; and offered her boiled barley.

"It's worse than children," Paddy said glumly. "We can't ride her too hard when she's not eating."

"Won't be riding her at all," Sam said miserably. "Zara—do eat up, please—come on now, it's good for you."

The mare tossed her head irritably. She was tired of being fussed. She was tired of winter. She wanted to run in a sunny meadow and eat new grass. She wanted to race, but not in the needling wind that knifed her whenever she went out for exercise.

"She's sickening for something," Sam said forlornly.

"Honest to God, boyo," Paddy said in exasperation, "take Tarzan out and exercise him. The mare'll catch your wully-grumbles and so will I."

Sam took Tarzan into the big field and walked him to loosen his muscles. He wanted to ride hard, to gallop against the wind, but the hunter needed careful exercising, having been cooped up too long, as had all the horses. It was colder than he had ever known it. His ears hurt, his face was stung by the wind, his hands were numb and could hardly feel the reins. Tarzan was uncooperative. He wanted his warm stable.

Richard rang that night to say that Stella had developed a cold. The operation could not take place until she was better. Meanwhile, she was in a private ward in the hospital, and they would be away for longer than he had expected.

He listened as Vence told him of the mare's sudden choosiness.

"Try feeding her at night," he suggested. "And take the record player into the stables. A few soothing long players might help her. 'Swan Lake'—and the Brahms 'Lullaby'—and if Sam's too nervous he'd better keep away till he's got over it. Horses are telepathic when it comes to moods."

Soft music and quiet was what Zara needed. She began to feed properly, but her management obsessed the men, and Paddy swore vigorously at Chris for watering her after her meal instead of before.

"You'll dilute her digestive juices," he said. "And you didn't let the water stand either. It's enough to chill her. I'll see to her in future."

"Everyone's as nowty as midges," Chris said irritably to Sarah, stabbing his fork savagely into a sausage.

"They've too much on their minds, love," Sarah said, comfortable as always. "Just make allowances. A lot depends on that mare—could make a lot of difference here if she wins."

Sam was the next to catch cold. Vence took over Zara's training. The schedule over her stall bit into his dreams.

Build her up and exercise her. He inspected the hay daily, almost prepared to sample it himself to make sure it was good. She was having fourteen pounds of it each day and nine pounds of best oats. She was not too keen on oats, but they were necessary to build her muscles. Paddy allowed no one but himself to prepare her warm feed.

He alternated two pounds of boiled rye with two pounds of boiled barley, and added a pound of boiled

peas, which he insisted must be two years old. Into this
he mixed half a pound of boiled linseed, half a pound
of steamed bran, a pound of steamed oats, and salt, and
two teaspoons of charcoal.

Sam and Chris, seeing this prepared for the first time,
watched him, grinning, their smiles growing ever
broader as he explained that the rye and peas, with a
layer of bran and crushed oats, should be covered and
left for two hours. Otherwise it would not swell until it
was inside the mare—and then there would be trouble.

"It's like a witch's brew," Chris said.

"He could say a spell," Sam suggested.

"Zara, Zara, eat your food,
Make it swell and make it good,
Zara, Zara, swallow up,
Or you'll sell us all a pup," Chris said, laughing.

"Honest to God," Paddy said, "will the two of you
get out of here and leave a man in peace? Ye don't jest
about sacred subjects—I've enough to do, and so have
you. There's work around here—or haven't ye noticed?"

Work. Stables to clean and feeds to prepare and
horses to groom. Water to fetch and hay to bring and
hay bags to fill. Horses to exercise. A colt with a tem-
perature and Midnight bad-tempered with weather.
Rain and frost and rain again. Stella's operation was
now scheduled to take place two days before the race.
Her cold had been the start of a bad bout of influenza.
She needed time to recover her strength.

Zara was taken out daily and walked around the
lanes. Whenever the ground was fit Jim Vence took her
over the fences they had built, with Paddy and Chris
riding beside her. She loved jumping, and she and Sam
had taught one another, practice leading to gradual
perfection.

The mare was in her pomp. Her coat glistened; her

muscles rippled under her skin, and passers-by, seeing her at exercise, stopped, enthralled. The villagers, knowing she was to run at Wetherby, began to eye her speculatively. Should she carry their money? Aaron knew she should, if only Sam could get rid of his miseries. Not like him to get nervous.

But as the days passed and the mare greeted him with brilliant eyes and tossing head, and a splendid show of energy, Sam's confidence returned. Nothing was going to happen to him or her. This was the crucial week, if only the mare could stand up to it. He looked at her week's exercise schedule.

Monday.   One and a half miles, half speed.

Tuesday.   Walking and trotting.

Wednesday.   Two miles, half speed.

Thursday.   Walking and trotting.

Friday.   Cantering and school.

Saturday.   Five-furlong gallop—fast.

He followed the schedule faithfully, walking home, high on her back, trim in breeches and jacket and hard hat. He was aware of eyes watching them. Zara reacted to admiration. She knew she was beautiful, and she stepped regally, head high, occasionally tossing her mane. Her sleek silken tail swished from side to side.

"Proud Mare—Proud Stud." The pun and play on the word became a village joke, a symbol of affection. She was theirs. Passers-by, dropping in for a drink in the Bell, asked about her. Zara, the Pride of Weeredale. A reporter saw her, but hugged his knowledge to himself. He intended to back her to win at Wetherby. She had the lines of a winner.

In that last week she and Sam cemented the bond between them. He had only to ask, and she granted his wishes. A touch on her reins was all that was needed.

Silk-mouthed and obedient, willing and brave-hearted,

she set herself to excel. Sam knew she could leave every horse in the stable standing, and when, for her final gallop, she raced against Jed's Ginger King and Blue Rocket, he knew she could have beaten both if he'd let her run flat out. He went to bed almost sick with excitement.

The race was two days away.

The race was tomorrow. Tomorrow, and the mare was as ready as ever she could be, and he was trained and fit and his weight was right. They were ready to run their best and try their hardest.

Tomorrow. He could never live through the dragging hours. He could not settle to any job, and twice Paddy swore at him for daydreaming.

"Race or no race, there's work to be done. Get on wi' it. Honest to God, boyo, you'll never make tomorrow if ye go on like that. Just get on and fill those buckets and mind ye let them stand."

It was eleven o'clock. In twenty-four hours they would already be on their way. Half-past eleven, and the day was endless, stretching to eternity, filled with an overwhelming weight of boredom.

Zara greeted him skittishly. He groomed her. She was full of herself, above herself, bursting with energy, the stable queen, petted and feted and adored. She turned her head and gave him a love nip on the hand that held the brush, drawing blood.

"You damn silly beast," Sam said crossly. "Don't do that again."

Paddy laughed.

"Honest to God, she can't wait for tomorrow," he said.

Twelve o'clock. The day had come to a standstill. Time had ceased to exist. All of them were impatient, eager for the passing hours.

Twelve-fifteen, and Richard rang to say Stella had had her operation yesterday. He had not yet seen her. As yet the surgeon could not be definite about the outcome. And how was the mare? Vence told him she'd nipped Sam, and he laughed.

"I hope she won't get too excited," he said. "She's feeling her oats."

"She'll be fine tomorrow, you'll see," Vence said, voicing a confidence he didn't feel.

"Don't count your winnings till she's past the post," Richard told him.

Vence grinned to himself.

One o'clock. Sam couldn't eat and he couldn't work. He went over to find Sue and try for comfort from Sarah. Paddy and Vence had forbidden him the stables lest he upset Zara. He was as restless as a kitten chasing its tail.

Zara. She was all they could think about. Vence peeped in at her a dozen times. She was feeding quietly. She eyed him and returned to the food.

"Honest to God," Paddy said. "We'll none of us make tomorrow at this rate!"

The afternoon before the race everyone was edgy. Sam snapped at Chris, and Sue, drifting from one room to another, waiting to hear from her father, who had promised to phone again when he had seen her mother, was unable to settle to any activity. She looked out at the moors and suddenly longed for a walk.

"Good idea," Sarah said. "Take the boys with you. Do Sam good and get his mind off tomorrow. He's eating nowt but pickin's, and got an appetite like a bird. He's a mass of nerves, and Chris isn't much better. Anyone'd think races had never been run before."

"Not this one," Sue said.

They took Rip, the farm sheepdog, with them, and Nan's young Doberman, Brutus. Sue, dressed in thick

trousers and an anorak, swung out beside the two boys.
She looked over the sweep and rise of the bleak moors,
along the Weere to the hill above, and to the stark trees
on the skyline.

"Have you ever seen the Weere Pot?" she asked
Chris.

He shook his head. He was glad to be out of the
house, which had seemed to be brooding, waiting for
news of Stella. The silent telephone menaced them, all
suddenly afraid of the news it might be bringing them.
Success was almost a certainty, the doctor had said, but
there was always a risk and that everyone knew. . . .
And no one knew either if the growth was harmless. It
could be malignant. There had been no point in hiding the truth. Sue was no longer a child, and the shock
might be greater if she thought all was well and it was
not.

The three cut off across the hill. They began to
climb, using the well-marked sheep trails that criss-
crossed the ground, picking out the easier places, so
that climbing was relatively easy. The beasts always
knew the best path to the top. Vence said that England
could be travelled from north to south by the beast
ways—fox and badger, deer and sheep and wild pony
marked every patch of countryside and farmland.

They crawled through the sheep tunnel that led from
one side of the high stone wall to the other, crouching
over rocks that cropped from the ground on either side.
A curlew whistled, softly trilling, quite unseen, an iso-
lated lonely cry that echoed the bleakness of sky and
ground, so that the three of them were conscious of the
grey winterblighted grass and the black thrust of leaf-
less branches into the sullen, ice-cold air.

Sam's thoughts, as they walked, were all of the race
tomorrow. He had been, often enough, to the course,

and two days before he and Vence had driven over and walked every inch of the way, noting the slope and lie and curve of the ground, planning the method of their race, trying to anticipate how Zara would react to so many other horses and to a crowd. Though if the day were cold there might be few enough there.

They reached the crest of the hill. Below them the village huddled in the dip, grey houses and greystone walls and a greystone church shielded by spiring yews. The square Norman tower looked squat from so high, and the Weere was a trickle between its banks, and the cars on the winding road were diminished by distance. A horse, wearing a New Zealand rug, cropped in a field by himself, and Frisian cattle moved to the stream and drank, black and white and reduced in size so that they seemed part of a doll's farm, unreal miniatures.

A kestrel hovered above them, and flew away. A blackbird sang a brief song from a near-by bush. Time had stopped, and they were marooned in a world devoid of other people, a world that had no boundaries and stretched on endlessly, the wide moors rolling until they came to the tempestuous sea, and the houses below them were a mirage, where no people lived. Deserted as a ghost town. Sue looked down spellbound, wondering if the boys echoed her thoughts, but Sam had no mind for anything but the mare and the race they would run tomorrow, and Chris was savouring the air and the pleasure of moving without more than a suggestion of a limp, and thinking of the tea that Sarah would have waiting for them when they returned.

"Let's have a quick look at the Pot and then get back," he said, and Sue was glad to be released from her spell, to return to reality, and to walk on, noting a hare that bounded out of a bracken patch and a gull flying overhead, come inland from bad weather.

The sheepdog chased rabbit smells, glad to be free from work for once and not called constantly to heel. Rip enjoyed a break from responsibility. Brutus, tagging behind him, gambolled after shadows and lolloped absurdly in his wake, so that Sue grinned, watching them.

"How much farther?" Chris asked, and Sue pointed to a jumble of rocks some five hundred yards away.

"That's one of the entrances. The main one's farther on. It's a famous place. You can get right along inside it, to a big limestone cave, and then there's a tunnel which leads out here. It's best to go in from the other end."

"You're not proposing to go in?" Chris said.

"Of course not. Or if we do, only a little way. We haven't got torches or anything. It'd be daft."

"So long as I know," Chris said.

They reached the crack in the ground and peered down it.

"How do you get down?" Chris asked.

"They've put rods in the rock . . . you can climb down on those," Sue said. "It's not a big drop . . . about twelve feet. It's pretty narrow. It wouldn't do to be fat."

"Best be getting back," Sam said. "We don't want to have to get home in the dark. It's not so easy to find your way by night across these slopes and I wouldn't care to try and get down the hill to the road then either. It's tricky going."

They whistled the dogs and turned back. A few minutes later Sue turned to look for Brutus, who had not followed them.

She called.

A long whimper came from the bracken. Rip ran back, and barked.

They raced to the bracken patch, and Sam parted it. A gaping crack led into the ground, and a long whine came from the bottom of the crack. Sue bent down and called again, and Brutus barked at her, his voice distant.

"He's fallen down. . . . He sounds as if he's miles below," she said miserably.

Chris dropped onto his face and peered into the darkness.

"It's as black as a peat bog," he said unhappily. "How far away's that tunnel end? They might be connected . . . . If one of us can get down to the dog and entice him out . . . he won't find his own way. He's too young and too soft."

"I wish we hadn't come," Sue said.

"What's the use of that, you idiot?" Chris said crossly. He ran over to the rocks that were tumbled at the tunnel end. "I can't get down here . . . . I'm too big."

"I can," Sam said.

"For goodness' sake be careful." She did not want anyone to go. They ought to go for help. One of the farms might be able to lend them torches or a man who would try and dig the dog out. . . . But he sounded as if he were too far down for that. Poor brute. . . . What the devil could they do?

Sam crawled into the tunnel. He was instantly blind. He had to rely on touch, on the feel of the rough damp-slimed walls, on the pressure of his hands over the uneven ground. He called softly, and faint and very far away he heard Brutus whine. If only the dog would come to him. If only the tunnel didn't branch. . . . He reached out his hand. The roof was higher, and he could stand up. He would have to go back for a torch . . . . He was being stupid. There was a wind past his face, and when he turned he could see the faint light at the tunnel entrance and the outline of the two heads watching him. He whistled again, and this time the dog's whine sounded closer, and he distinctly heard the sound of padding paws and claws clicking on stone.

He reached out and found a gap in the wall. He could turn right, or keep straight on. He whistled in the gap. The sounds came from straight in front of him, and Brutus, sure that help was near, began to bark, the echoes reverberating noisily from walls and floor and roof.

"Brutus!" he called, and the barks stopped, and once more he heard the dog move towards him, following the sound of his voice. He went towards the animal, and next moment his foot slipped and he tripped over a rock that lay on the ground in front of him, an unseen trap in the dark. He took three swift steps as he fought to recover his balance, and a moment later his feet slid from under him and he was glissading down a steep slope, unable to stop himself from falling. He landed with a bump that jarred his bones, and a second later the dog was standing beside him, licking his face in frantic welcome, whining softly, pleased tail creating a draught.

"Sam," Chris was calling from somewhere far above. "Where the hell are you?"

"The devil only knows," Sam answered ruefully. "I've slipped into some sort of shaft. The sides are like glass. Brutus is here with me. I can't see a thing."

That was no exaggeration. The darkness was tangible, terrifying, and oppressive, blanketing his eyes and hiding reality. He knew there was stone all about him, sloping steep walls, slimed with moisture, smelling of age-old damp, musty and unpleasant. There was water underfoot. And, quite suddenly, he knew where he was. He was in the Little Pot, the trap that, when the rains came or the snow melted, filled with water to the brim, and last year had drowned two cavers who had been caught there and had fallen as he had. And they had been properly equipped, not come like tomfools without lights or ropes or food. No one had been able to get to them in time. The Pot filled in a matter of minutes . . . there was a stream that led in somewhere underground. He was conscious of the trickle and drip of water, of the seep through his shoes, of the sound and murmur of an unseen spring. His mouth was dry, and he felt sick.

"I'm in the Little Pot," he yelled.

There was an appalled silence.

"What's that?" Chris asked.

Sue stared at him, her eyes enormous, fear-filled.

"He can't get out without ropes. It's about ten feet deep, with steep sides. And they can't get to him from this side. . . . They'll have to go through from the Weere Pot itself. . . . There isn't room to work with ropes in the tunnel Sam went down. It'll take them about four hours to get to him. . . . And then they've got to get him out. And it's bitter cold in there . . . and if it rains the Pot fills up in twenty minutes. . . . He'll drown."

"Then shut up and get moving," Chris yelled at her. "For God's sake go and get help. You know the way and I don't. And run . . . it's clouding over and it's already three o'clock. . . . They won't get to him before dark. . . . Get someone to phone Sarah. . . . I'll stay here and lend moral support."

"You won't try to go in?" Sue asked. She thought of Sam alone in the dark and the rainstorms growing, building up in the sky, and began to shake.

"Not on your life. One damned idiot is enough. . . . We should have left the dog. . . . Get going. . . ."

Sue began to run.

"Don't run . . . walk," Chris called after her. "No good if you break a leg. . . . Just keep moving."

It was all very well to talk. Rip followed her, and she was glad of his company. It was lonely on the moors, and though there were rarely strangers about, her father did not like her walking alone. There were some nasty stories told on dark nights in the safety of the fire-lit room or in the warm companionable glow in the Bell. She had heard one or two from Paddy, who thought she should be warned against the evils that lay in wait for the unwary, and Paddy, who had an Irishman's love of a good story well told, saw that his horrors lost nothing in the telling.

The curlew's plangent call was a plaint that tore at the springs of fear. Only she and the bird were alive in the world, and help was distant. She did not know whether to run first and try the farm. Everyone might be out and the house locked so that she could not telephone. It was Sunday afternoon, and the chores would be done, and sometimes the farm folk visited relatives in Huddersfield. Better to go to the village. The vicar was sure to be there, in the vicarage that nestled among the trees beyond the church. He would be thinking of his evening sermon and enjoying a quiet Sunday afternoon, unless there was a christening.

The hillside had never seemed so steep, and she missed the path that led to the tunnel between the fields. She climbed the stone wall, clinging to rocky outcrops that hurt her hands. Rip whined at her and then barked, as the jump was too high for him. As she dropped to the other side, he streaked away and found the gap and ran through and raced back to join her, panting. The quickest way down was to slither and slide beside the bed of a dry steam where the tumbled rocks were heaped in profusion and the banks were slimed with mud.

She could think of nothing but Sam and the dog, both deep underground. If only she hadn't wanted a walk. . . . If only she hadn't brought them to the Weere Pot, if only she had remembered the cracks and gullies that laced the hill, one leading into another, a winding wilderness of limestone tunnels that annually led adventurers to danger and four times to her knowledge had led to death.

Her breath was sobbing in her throat, her heart thumping, and her legs aching. The village was nearer, but the greystone houses looked grim and unwelcoming. The fields were divided into strips, each length high-walled, and at the end of each was a stout stone barn. Yorkshire was prolific with its building materials, and the old ways of farming and landowning still survived the usage of centuries. She had four more walls to climb, and then she would have to cross the Weere, and it was running deeper than usual. There was no time to get to the bridge. She glanced at her watch. She had already been walking for half an hour, and darkness was a breathing space away. If only she had never suggested the damn-fool expedition. . . . She would never forgive herself if anything happened to Sam and the dog.

"Please, God," she whispered under her breath. "Please, God. Please, God."

She would never be so stupid again. If only they were safe. . . . Please, God. She was slipping on the grass, which was damp from a shower of rain a few hours before. Please, God. How long did the stream take to fill so that it flooded the Little Pot? Please, God, let them be safe. . . . Let me be in time. . . . Don't let it rain. . . .

Her whirling thoughts were interrupted by a shout. She stopped, terrified, and looked about her. It had been a man's voice. Rip, beside her, was poised, listening, ears pricked, one forepaw lifted and curled.

"Sue . . ."

She breathed a deep sigh of relief. It was the shepherd from Broken Wall Farm. His daughter Mary was a friend of hers, and she went there sometimes to tea. She waited for him, her legs suddenly trembling, and as he came up and Rip ran to greet his dog Tizz, she was horrified to find herself in tears.

Joe Gregg was beside her in a second.

"What's oop, love? Is it your mam?"

Sue stared at him, shocked. She had forgotten her mother . . . had forgotten all about the operation. Her father would have telephoned and she wasn't even there. All she could do was shake her head.

"There's no man after you?" Joe could not imagine why she was in such distress. It wasn't like Sue. Self-contained little thing, not like his Mary who was all pepper and fire and temper and never in the same mood for two seconds together. But there, the Prouds had had a lot of trouble one way and another this past year or two, and not surprising if the lass lost her balance.

"Sam . . . and Brutus . . ." Sue could hardly speak for sobs. "They're in the Little Pot."

Joe needed no more to tell him of urgency. He took a notebook and pencil from his pocket and wrote on it, and then fastened the note to Tizz's collar.

"Find Bob, fast," he said, and Tizz streaked down the hill and through the sheep gap and was gone from their sight.

"He's used to carrying messages for me," Joe said. "Needs to be out on these hills. Bob's my brother-in-law. He'll be at home now and he's got a telephone. Tizz'll be there in no time. Now, lass, dry oop and try and tell me about it."

Sue wiped her eyes and began to relax. Even though

she often felt that adults had little to recommend them, it was comforting to have one around in a real emergency. Joe had taken over entirely. There was nothing more that she could do.

"I've some coffee with me," Joe said, taking a flask from the deep pocket of the capacious overcoat that he always wore. A shepherd needed a great deal of equipment, one way and another, and as well as food and drink he carried iodine and marking sticks and ear notchers and a plastic mat to kneel on when the ewes were lambing; though none of his Blackfaces was due yet, you never knew at this time of the year, and if he saw another man's sheep in trouble he would always help. He also carried wire cutters. There was little wire, but there was some down by the Weere, and sheep could get tangled up, and it wasn't easy to get the stuff out of their fleeces. Scared by a strange dog, they might not look where they were going.

He looked up at the sky. Like all shepherds he was way-wise and weather-wise, and there was rain coming, though not yet. The trouble was that the stream that flooded the Little Pot was fed from the other side of the hill, and it might well be that it was raining over there; there was no way of telling. He hated the Little Pot. He had been there when the two kids were drowned last year. They were all the same, the youngsters. Went in blind without a thought in their silly heads. If that pair had only used their wits they would still be alive, as they had failing batteries in their torches. They committed every crime in the book. They separated and went on alone, and, tracking one another by sound, had both slipped into the Pot. The sides were like glass. And it had rained that day, God, how it had rained. There had been a thunder-storm. . . . He would never forget that afternoon, standing, soaked to

the skin, as flash after flash lit the hill and the slow rescue went on, the men crawling through miles of tunnel
in the darkness, and he thought of the crash and echo
of thunder, deep underground, the slow sullen rumble,
and the deadly creep and trickle of the seeping water
until the spring suddenly overflowed and death came
swiftly, mercilessly, and icily.

They brought out the two youngsters in the darkness
and he had looked at the dead faces, the pair of them
no older than his own lad Tom, and thought bitterly of
the waste . . . the blind wicked waste. The young
seemed to have a suicide impulse built into them.
Though after all, Sam had gone to rescue the dog, and
that wasn't suicide, it was just the sort of damn-fool
thing Sam would do. Joe watched Sue drink and
thought of Sam, who was courting Mary, he was pretty
sure, and he waited for the first Land Rover to roar
down the village street, shattering the Sunday silence.
He had food too, which he gave to her, and she nibbled
at it, her mind unable to think of anything but Sam
down there in the dark, her eyes on the distant clouds
that threatened them all.

"First Land Rover, and there goes the second," Joe
said a moment later in satisfaction. "Tizz's delivered his
message. Let's get back to Chris and call to Sam that
rescue's on its way. Could he hear you and answer
you?"

"Just about," Sue said drearily. She was too tired to
think, and she could not take her eyes off the banking
clouds. She knew how fast the Little Pot filled. "What
did you say in your note?"

"That Sam and Nan's dog were trapped in the Little
Pot." Joe whistled, and a black and white shape
streaked towards him through the dead bracken. "Here,
Tizz. Good dog. Good lad then, fine fellow."

He patted the dog, meting generous praise, and Rip, jealous, butted at Sue's leg so that she stopped and stroked him too. The two dogs fell in behind them, plumed tails waving. Joe had detached a note from the dog's collar. He handed it to Sue.

"Alerted rescue team. Taking track up to Weere Pot. Will be inside before you get back. Sent message to Sarah Vence."

"They were quick," Sue said.

"You learn to be quick," Joe answered. He squeezed her arm. "They'll have him out in no time, lass."

"In four hours. And there's rain coming," Sue said. She looked up at the sky. Soon darkness would overwhelm them and Sam would still be down there and it would be raining. She plodded on up the hill, and for a few moments, all around her, the curlew call sounded, eerie and lonely as the birds wheeled in the air, and desolation filled her. She'd killed Sam through her own stupidity, and she would never be able to live with herself in the future. She was useless, futile, stupid. She berated herself brutally.

"Don't worry, lass," Joe said, watching her face. He knew he could not comfort her. Poor little devil. She just had to learn the way they all did, by bitterness and misery. Could never learn any other way. You never believed it till it happened to you. . . . It was a hard cruel world, and the kids had it harder than ever these days, easy meat for every crook and shyster. Young, impressionable, and idealistic, not yet having developed the cynicism that would protect those that survived. Not realizing that others lived to prey on them, to prey on their greed or their hopes or their fears, to bolster faint hearts with drugs that rotted them, to entice their money from them. He wanted to protect his Mary and little Sue, but he couldn't even give them advice. They

wouldn't listen. Wouldn't ever know that their parents
watched them and suffered. As his wife did every time
Tom rushed out on his motor bike and came home
bragging of his narrow escapes, the swaggering hero dic-
ing with death, exaggerating every escapade, so damned
sure of himself, and laughing. His mother didn't laugh.

Chris was waiting for them, huddled against the rock.
He had been calling to Sam, but his voice was failing
and his throat ached. It was not easy to yell at the top
of his pitch for so long.

"Rescuers should have started down the tunnel by
now," Joe said. He nodded to the Land Rovers which
were parked some hundreds of yards away, at the main
entrance to the Weere Pot. Dusk was masking the
moors, and distance had become deceptive. Below them
lights patched the village street and marked the position of a few of the houses, and light shone from the
church, a soft serene glow reflecting a place untroubled
by anxiety, spelling sanctuary and peace.

The wind was rising, moaning in the stunted bushes.
Joe took Chris's place and called to Sam, who called
back, his voice fainter. He was bitterly cold, even with
the dog huddled against him. He was glad they were together and Brutus, although unhappy because of the
cold and the dark, and hungry with the savage appetite
of youth and health, was content to lean against Sam,
acknowledging his company and comfort, occasionally
licking the boy's hand to show his gratitude that someone had come to share his curious imprisonment.

Sam was sitting on a flat rock that projected from the
ground and was above the water, which was over half
an inch deep. He had managed to find room for the
dog beside him, but his shoes were in water, and his
feet were icy. All around him was the soft swish and
trickle, the seep and drip and slither reminding him of

the filling stream, and he wondered if it was raining outside but he dared not ask. Help was coming. Joe had said so, but help had to come from the Weere Pot, and it was a tortuous and twisting route that they had to travel, descending several steep drops, burrowing through the atrociously narrow Cripples' Passage, where it was only possible to move flat on your face. Sam had been as far as there just once, and had gone back, longing for the open air. The familiar sensation of smothering suddenly came on him, and he set his teeth and put both arms round the dog for comfort. It was his childhood nightmare, flaring to reality, to be alone and buried in the dark.

It was a fear from long ago, before man was civilized, a fear from the days of cavemen when horrors lurked inside and outside at night and creatures could come silently from the depths of the hill and inflict death. As the water might come. . . . For a moment he could hear it, hear the sound gathering in volume, hear the murmur rise to a roar, a death threat, and he stopped thinking and held his breath, waiting for the sudden final rush that would cover him and the dog and leave them drowned and perhaps not caring. What happened when a man died? Was that the end? Or did something last? Some remnant of memory—he had never wondered before.

He did not want to die. He wanted to live to go and see Mary Gregg tomorrow after the race and tell her that Zara had won. He wanted to be back with the mare in the warm comfort of her stable, surrounded by familiar people and places and steeped in the horse smell that always excited him, making him think of racing over the turf, the swiftest horse in the world beneath him.

The sounds were louder. He switched his thoughts deliberately to the race-course at Wetherby and set out, mentally, to walk it again, inch by inch, knowing how much depended on the weather and whether the going was good or soft, or heavy. Zara did not like soft running. She was a fastidious little creature, and hated mud on her legs. All female. When they put her to the stallion . . . there would be a foal to end all foals, and he would not be there to see it, or to school it, or to ride it.

The sounds were louder, echoing and uncanny. There was running water coming fast through the maze of passages, coming towards him, ready to fill and flood the Pot. He could do nothing but wait.

Above him on the hillside Sue was watching the lights of the Land Rovers. Three men stood outside the Weere Pot, and six men had gone in. They had brilliant lights and they had packs with food and blankets. And they had a stretcher. Sam hadn't said he was hurt. . . . If they got him out and he couldn't race tomorrow—

A voice spoke, and she jumped.

"Arrah, sweetheart," Paddy said reproachfully. She turned to him, and tears came back into her eyes and streaked her cheeks so that he hurriedly put out his torch and put his arm round her. "Come on now, it's only Paddy. They'll have the boyo out in no time, honest to God, they're used to rescue work. Here, Sarah sent some soup for you and Chris, and some pasties, and your dad phoned again and your mam's tumour wasn't malignant at all, it was quite harmless, and they say your mam will be better than new in a week or so, and your dad's flying up to Leeds tomorrow, and we're meeting him to take him to Wetherby. He can fly back to London in time to see your mam, and no point in him staying in the hotel mooning about. He can't see her till seven-thirty. Vence suggested it, and honest to God it was a brain wave."

The words were spilling out of Paddy in an effort to

stop Sue's tears, but when he had finished she buried her face in his shoulder and cried more bitterly.

"Arrah, sweetheart," he said, sure she would do herself harm.

"Dad'll fly up and Sam won't be there . . . or won't be fit to ride," she managed to say at last, and Paddy tightened his hold on her. He had daughters too, and his Mollie was the same age as Sue and quite as difficult to handle.

Far away, from the churchyard, came the low call of a hunting owl, and as they listened in the darkness the first thin drops of rain slid from the hidden sky and wetted the ground, and inside, crawling towards the Little Pot, the rescuers were increasingly conscious of the dreaded sound of running water.

Mercifully, Sam no longer heard. He had curled up on the damp rock, his head on the dog's back, and both he and Brutus were sound asleep, unaware of the sibilant threatening murmur that might, at any moment, become a roar and come crashing over them, bringing the end of both their worlds.

CHAPTER *thirteen*

There was nothing to do but wait. Wait in the darkness, listening to the sounds from the rescuers, who had
rigged up a walkie-talkie system. There were two policemen there now, who had come to see if further help
was needed, and a number of men from the village had
joined them. They stood in small groups, and the only
friendly sight was the dim and glow of pipe and cigarette as they drew on them, and the patched orange
windows of the houses below, speaking of warmth, and
of safety.

The rain was a thin drizzle, a grim reminder of the
filling stream that thrust and probed and drove its way
deep underground, Sue could not go home, although
the policemen had offered to drive her. She sat in the
Land Rover, huddled in an old coat belonging to her
father, and listened to the faint whisper of rain against
the windscreen and the roof, and shivered. Time had
ceased. She was marooned by desperation, by nagging
insistent fear, in an existence without a past or a future.
She caught sight of Annie Lethwaite standing at the entrance to the Weere Pot, her face haggard. She had not
thought of Annie before, and she did not want to meet
her or to speak to her. She did not know what to say.

Chris, beside her, had nothing to say either. He could not comfort her or himself. He wished that they had let him take part in the rescue. The night seemed endless.

Annie was numb with cold and with fear. She had lived too long in the Dale not to know the danger of the Little Pot. She had never thought to see her own son there. Just like Sam to go down after a fool dog. Slow tears slid from her eyes. All these years. Were they all to be wasted? The long-ago misery when she knew she was to have a child . . . a payment for her wildness. She had reformed completely, all her passion turning into mother love, and she had fought and worked for Sam ever since. She had been delighted when he started work at the Proud stud, among the horses, a much better sort of job than errand boy in a supermarket. She had a countrywoman's respect for work among beasts, and the town held no pleasure for her any more.

She stared into the darkness, feeling rain against her face, and both she and Sue echoed one another's thoughts in agonized prayer. Please, God. Please, God. I'll never do it again if you only let Sam live . . . the old childhood prayers. I'll be a good girl if you don't let them find out.

There were other women on the hill now. They all knew Sam. They had come, unable to sit in their quiet homes, as soon as they heard that he was trapped. There was unity in fear, and all of them had sons or daughters. One of the women had a flask of tea with her, and she gave Annie a drink. She had no words of comfort, but the gesture was enough and warmed Annie as much as the tea.

Some minutes later Aaron and Adam came up the hill together and joined Paddy and Jim Vence, who nodded to them briefly when they spoke.

"No news?" Aaron said, his voice hoarse. His grandson was suddenly important to him. He had never real-ized how much the lad meant until they brought thenews to the cottage. He stared at the entrance to the Pot.Black, forbidding, a tumble of rock, the entrance to apit that was frightening as the underworld. More so, forit had reality in this world, not in a problematical after-life. Old Adam, standing behind him, blew on hishands and huddled into his coat. It was icy on the hill. . . poor lile nazzart, down there in the bitter-colddark. . . .

Inside the tunnel the men were conscious of time.Time and weather. Neither was on their side. Thestream did not threaten the rescuers. It flooded in onthe other side of the Little Pot, but its noise waslouder, no longer murmurous, but a deeper throatyrumble, so that Dave Lowrie, who led the rescue, andwho preached in the chapel further down the Dale onSundays, was reminded of the Psalms, the Revelationof St. John. . . .

"His voice is as the sound of many waters."

He added his own prayers to those that Annie andSue sent up. He had rescued the two drowned boys andhelped to bring them out into the air again. It was hardto forget that time . . . and he had two young sons ofhis own.

The policemen had sons too. They waited and lis-tened, as they so often waited and listened. Routine wasmostly dull, and their presence a deterrent rather thana threat on many occasions. They could do withoutsuch incidents as this. Sam was a decent lad. . . .

At home Nan sat with Sarah, the television setturned on, but neither of them saw the pictures thatwere flashed into the room. Jack Braithwaite had notgone to join the others after the cattle were safelylocked up for the night and the horses fed. He had promised Vence and Paddy that he would take care of everything. He went to look at Zara. He had wagered his money on her, in an ante-post bet, and Paddy had staked one hell of a lot . . . and even if they did get Sam out in time it looked as if he would not be fit to ride . . . or if he did, he would be far from fit enough to win. It was a gruelling job, and not one for those who were not at their peak of health. Their money was as good as lost. No stakes returned on ante-post bets if the horse didn't run.

Out on the moor, Jim Vence climbed into the Land Rover. Sue had fallen asleep, her head on Chris's shoulder, and Chris had put his arm round her. He was looking at her face, lit by the edge of the glow from the two rescue Land Rovers that flooded their lights into the mouth of the tunnel. Sue moved and curled more closely, and Chris, surprised at his own reaction, felt a sudden fierce protectiveness and stooped to kiss her hair. Vence did not move. He had had no desire to play gooseberry, had never even guessed that the wind blew in that direction, and did not wish to be discovered.

Far away, from beneath their feet, Brutus barked. Sue woke instantly, and there was a movement from the watchers at the tunnel mouth. If the dog was still alive, then there was not yet water in the Little Pot. Vence slipped out of the back of the Land Rover, wondering why the dog had barked. Had he heard the rescuers? Or was the first trickle of water becoming a flood that alerted him to terror?

"They've reached the Pot," one of the men at the tunnel mouth said. "The water's rising; but Sam and the dog are okay. If they can fix the ropes before the flood bursts . . . . it comes in with a mighty rushing. . . ."

Sam was dazzled by light. He was numb with long hours spent crouched on the rock, and the dog was cold

too, and shivering. Sam had woken when Brutus
barked, and realized with a wave of thankfulness that
there were men's voices near. A moment later one of
them had called to him and been answered by a frenzy
from the dog that Sam could not silence. The sound
was deafening in so small a space. A good job the tunnel roof wasn't loose. . . .

"Can you hitch this?" a voice called down, and a can-
vas sling dangled towards him. He managed to fix it
round the dog. He was aware of the sound of water,
now intensified, and desperately afraid that the sudden
rush and swirl would come before they returned the
sling to him. But he could not go first and leave the
dog, as that would mean that someone else would have
to be lowered into the Pot. He watched Brutus swing
into the air, frantic paws flailing at nothing, a thin unhappy whimper sounding eerily in the shaft. Above, a
reassuring voice tried to comfort the animal.

There was a runnel of water foaming over the edge.
The level in the Little Pot rose to his ankles, and he
watched the white froth gather, a sickness in his throat.
The dog was released, and the sling dropped towards
him, and he fastened it with trembling hands, shivering. The rope tightened, and he braced his feet against
the slimy wall and gasped as he rose slowly upwards
and the runnel became a pouring flood.

He was level with his rescuers.

"Quick," a voice said, and they were pulling him
through the cave, up into the tunnel, climbing fast,
until they reached the Cripples' Passage and could see
where the water marked the walls, and that they were
above the highest level.

"Through the passage, and then we'll warm you up,"
Dave said, more than thankful to have both boy and
dog safe. The dog was walking happily beside his res-

cuer, who had tied a handkerchief through his collar.

Sam was so cold that he thought he would never know warmth again. The rough floor of the Cripples' Passage was torment to his hands. His chattering teeth rattled so loudly that he thought the men at the tunnel entrance must hear. The dog was shivering too.

Brutus was afraid of the passage. He did not understand that he must wriggle through, flattened to the ground. Someone thrust him down and pushed, and Sam called, until at last, whimpering with fear, the dog pushed his body through and hands reached out to pull him the last foot, so that he erupted into the cave and greeted Sam as if they had been separated for centuries.

"Dry clothes, a hot drink, and onto the stretcher," Dave said.

"I'm all right," Sam protested.

"No hot drink," a voice said.

One of the policemen had come to join them.

"Not yet. He's probably suffering from exposure. Just warm him up."

Sam was glad to lie on the stretcher with the blankets warm around him. Behind them the surge of water was a foaming torrent, the roar and thud and thunder deafening, and the fear that had lain dormant suddenly leaped to life, a fear that even here, where they knew they were safe, the stream might change the habit of years and unleash its fury and drown them all.

Brutus was beside him, licking his face. Then the stretcher was lifted, and he watched the light in front of him illumine the secret places of the Weere Pot, shine on the gleam and slime of walls dank with moisture, shine on the outer cave where the air was dry and the walls glistened with crystals, diamond faced, that glinted in the glim.

Then came the wind on his cheek and the trickle of

rain, and the lightening of anxiety on the faces of those
who waited patiently for his release.

"It's almost midnight," a voice said.

Midnight. The church clock struck, the sound lingering in the air at each stroke. Conversation broke out, a sudden excited chatter, and Sue climbed stiffly out of the Land Rover and went to Sam. The doctor was bending over him.

"He's tough, this one," the doctor said. He stood up and pushed the dense thatch of white hair back from his forehead. "A good sleep, and he won't suffer. Put him to bed and I'll see him in the morning."

"I'm racing tomorrow," Sam said.

"I doubt that."

Sam sat up, pushing back the blankets.

"I'm racing. I'm riding the mare . . . she's ready and fit, and I don't care what happens to me. I'm going to ride."

"We'll see in the morning. I'll come and look at you at nine o'clock. How will that do? I'll let you ride if you're recovered, and I promise I won't stop you if I think you can make it. Now go home and sleep. Okay?"

Sam nodded.

"We'll take him home with us, Annie," Vence said. "Less travelling in the morning."

Annie nodded.

"So long as I know he's safe," she said. She ruffled her son's damp hair, and for once he did not glare at her but smiled up sleepily, reminding her of earlier days when he had been a little lad and she had been so necessary to him. "I'm coming to see you win," she said, and wandered off downhill without waiting for anyone else, a big untidy woman, who had that night been made happier than she believed possible. Her Sam was safe, and her spirits lifted, so that she sang softly, under her breath, as she made for the track and the slow way home.

Sam was asleep before they reached the house, but he woke when the Land Rover stopped, and demanded food, and Sue and Chris ate with him, and the dog bolted his meal and lay by the fire, sighing deeply, glad to be warm and safe and once more with friends. Long after he had gone to sleep, his legs twitched, and twice he whimpered and woke and made sure he was in his own home and not lying in the dark and the cold with cramped legs and hunger pangs so fierce that he did not know how to endure them, but licked again and again at the slime in the pit into which he had fallen.

Sue had nightmares too. She woke, terrified, after running through endless dark, and dressed herself and found a book and sat by the fire, while Brutus put his head on her foot and gained comfort from her presence. She watched the dawn creep across the Dale, burnishing the Weere, which was swollen and swift, scarcely contained between its banks, forging towards the village, wickedness in its wake.

CHAPTER *fourteen*

Sam was stiff when he woke. He slipped out of bed and went to the window, and saw the Weere and shuddered. Another hour in the Little Pot . . .

He looked up at the sky. The rain had ceased, and the glow on the horizon promised good weather. No sign of frost. He dressed and went downstairs. Sue had fallen asleep in her chair, and he grinned and quieted Brutus's extravagant greeting and went into the day.

Paddy was busy in the stable.

"I want one of the horses to ride," Sam said. "I'm stiff . . . need loosening up. What are you doing with Zara?"

"I'll walk her round the yard. Jim says we need to leave about ten-thirty. Your race is at three. No need to break our necks to get there. It's not that far. And eat some breakfast boyo, and don't be too far away when the doctor comes, or he'll be mad with you. Honest to God, can't leave you youngsters alone for a minute but you're in some sort of mischief. Arrah, get off wi' you, and don't go and break your neck. Canter Tarzan round the top field a time or two."

It was cold enough to send plumes of breath from their mouths, cold enough for a faint riming on bark and leafbud, cold enough for the grass to be crisply grey and the birds to sit huddled and fluffed, waiting for the sun. Cold enough to fire cheek and chill hand, and sting eyes. Cold enough for the horse to shy suddenly at a spiderweb glistening ghostily in the hedge, unexpected and uncanny, shaking as the spider scuttled across the threads.

Sam rode into the yard as the doctor drove his car through the gate. He saw Sam and grinned.

"I wish all my patients were like you," he said. "Or maybe not. I'd be out of a job."

He went to pat Zara.

"You'd better put ten shillings on her for me. Stiff after your adventure?"

"No more than after I've had a toss," Sam said. Tosses from horses were a fairly frequent occurrence, especially when he was schooling the colts. The bay three-year-old had a rare old temper and hated anyone on his back, even now. He would turn into a rogue if they didn't watch him. Not like Zara. He went to her, and she turned her head and rubbed against his shoulder.

"I hope she loves the stallion as much as she does you, Sam," Vence said, coming over from Midnight's stable.

"I'll wish you all luck, and be on my way," the doctor said. "I hear that Mrs. Proud stood the operation remarkably well."

"Mr. Proud rang us yesterday," Vence said. "He's flying up to see the race, as he can only visit his wife between seven-thirty and eight in the evening. There's a flight back from Leeds at five-thirty. Seems silly to hang around London. . . ."

"You won't know her when she comes home," the doctor said. "Good luck."

He drove off down the lane, a small, quiet man, dedicated to his patients and sadly overworked. If only he had thought, he might have realized what was wrong with Stella Proud much sooner . . . but a man rarely knew all the facts. He sighed. Life was a permanent predicament, like sailing in shoal waters. Sailing was his passion, and he knew all about that.

Sam had not expected the sudden build-up of exhilaration that seized him in the middle of breakfast. He was unable to eat a single mouthful. He drank his coffee and wondered if anyone else could sense his fleeting heart. His hands were hot, and he was afraid . . . afraid that he could not do justice to the mare, that his skill would desert him when he got on her back, that he would do something stupid like forgetting to weigh in, that when he looked at the other jockeys, at the men who had been his heroes, he would lose his nerve and run. They knew so much more than he knew.

But none of them was riding Zara.

Paddy and Vence had accustomed her to the horse-box and had driven her round the lanes. She stood, handsome in her blanket, waiting quietly as Paddy brought the box into the yard. Honey waited with her. The pair were inseparable, and the mare was never happy if the donkey was not there. There was room for two horses in the box. Adam and Aaron and Nan and her husband had all come to see them off and wish them luck. Chris was driving Sue and Sarah. Sam was travelling with Paddy and Vence. He had never imagined that excitement could be so intense. All his life he had waited for this day, for this chance, for this mare. . . . He sat silent as a shadow, scarcely daring to breathe, praying in his own way that nothing would happen to spoil their day, that they would reach the race-course safely, that no half-witted clot would crash into the horse-box. Paddy drove as if Zara were made of glass. They eased round the corners, anxious to protect her from even the slightest bump, and every ten miles they checked her and found her standing, patient, waiting for them to release her. At last Vence could bear it no longer, and he climbed into the double horse-box with Honey. He could watch Zara and gentle her and reassure her and see for himself that she had no bumps.

They stopped three miles from the course for sandwiches, and Sam managed to chew two mouthfuls, but he wanted nothing. He dared not drink more than a few sips, sure he would feel sick. Zara could not be fed till after the race.

They resumed their journey, and for Sam every moment took on the quality of a dream, so that he walked and spoke automatically, unable to believe that he was really living through the most enthralling experience of his life. Long afterwards, when he had more races to his credit than months to his age, he would resavour the feel of that first time, every moment of it vivid in remembrance, although on the actual day he had scarcely known what he was doing.

The race-course was familiar, and yet seemed suddenly strange. He had been there so often, but never like this. He watched Paddy and Vence bring the mare out of her box, and he saw people come up to her, admiring her. She tossed her head and looked at them out of the corners of her eyes, but did not bother about them, which was a good sign. She was handsomer than any of the other horses there. Her lines were exquisite.

The dreamlike feeling became even more fantastic when he went to weigh in. He, Sam Lethwaite, was going to be a jockey. A real jockey. He would become an apprentice . . . and one day he might even ride for the Queen. It was better to daydream than to speculate on the race or to wonder what the others thought of him. He was conscious of their glances, perhaps amused, perhaps weighing him up in his turn, wondering what horse he rode and who he was riding for and whether he presented any kind of competition. He was grateful to his valet, a small bent man with a kindly face and a limp, who knew, from experience, how it felt to ride in your first race, and who reassured him with a smile and a few brief words and sent him out with a hearty wish for good luck.

Everything seemed odd. He could not even now believe that he, Sam Lethwaite, was actually riding in a race. He had worn his racing colours before so that Zara was used to them, and the other lads at the stable who rode with him at exercise had worn bright colours too, yet they felt unfamiliar. Vence and Richard had done everything in their power to ensure that today nothing was unusual for Sam or the mare, although it was their first time out.

Vence had spent hours with the form book, assessing the opposition, and finally entered her, not among novices, but to run against others of her age, in the hope that she might not only show how she shaped in competition with tried horses, but would benefit from the fact that she was with experienced animals. She might get hurt contending with a green entry that did not know its job.

The unreality continued long after Zara was saddled, and Sam rode her with the other horses to loosen her up, making sure that she did not show a hint of her pace as she cantered freely. She was moving well, her head was cocked, her ears alert, her eyes eager. She looked curiously at a blinkered mare that passed her, and turned to gaze at Sam as if to ask him what on earth this curious furnishing was on the other animal's head. He patted her neck and spoke to her softly, and his familiar voice was reassuring. He hoped she would not sense his nervousness. His mouth was dry. He settled his cap, eased himself in the saddle, and rode up to join the others at the starting line.

Zara was used to other horses beside her. She gazed at them inquisitively, knowing they were strangers, and turned her head to seek for Honey, who was standing with Vence beside her, causing a small commotion of her own. Honey was in sight, and Vence and Paddy were there, and Sue and Chris. All her familiar people. She turned away, contented, aware of Sam, waiting for his signal, knowing that she was expected to run.

A moment later they were off. There was no time for fear. In front of them were scudding hooves, and behind them the sound of drumming legs. The rail was on his left, the faces behind it a blur that flashed and was gone, and there was nothing in the world but the churned-up grass and the flying feet and the pant and strain and pull of the racing horses.

He was lying fifth and was against the rails, how he did not know, having driven the mare there by instinct, an instinct that had come to him from his father, who had never failed to take advantage of an opportunity, however slight.

The ground was not too soft, and Zara did not heed the going, but watched the horses in front of her, knowing that they should not be there, that she could lead the field, that she ought to be in front, and that Sam was holding her back, preventing her from making her utmost effort, asking her to run slowly and carefully, telling her not to force her way through.

The fence in front, glimpsed at a distance, grew as they thundered towards it. She was eyeing it, weighing up her approach, and Sam eased the reins and let her drop her head as she rose to meet it, and they were up and flying and over, swift and easy as a swooping swallow, and she had recovered her stride and was third in the field and chasing to the second fence, excitement mastering her.

She did not need to be asked to jump. She loved jumping. It was in her blood and she knew what to do, and the hands on her reins were lighter than a feather touch, and Sam was easy in the saddle and rode as if he belonged to her, and she was barely conscious of his weight. Up and over and on, and the next fence looming, and she was still third, and the need to give her best and to go on and take the front of the field was urgent in her, and Sam found her hard to hold, and became, in the same moment, aware of his aching muscles, stiff from the previous day's adventure.

He set his mouth, and they were over the fence, and the sound of hooves and of the wind past his ears was as noisy as the rush and roar of the raging torrent, and the flash of the rail at his side was a white blur, scarcely glimpsed, and the other horses were mirages, and only he and the mare existed.

Up and over and on, catching the second horse, running neck and neck, hearing the cry of the crowd as a horse and jockey fell behind them, hugging the rails to gain ground and keep up with the leaders, and on to the next fence and over. Up and over and on.

There were people crowding, watching them. The first horse was one of the best of her year, and the second had won several races, but Zara was holding her own with ease, and there was plenty of running left in her, and she knew that she must go on and take the lead, must keep up with these two mares that were running away in front, must do as Sam asked. Vence, his glasses focused on her, watched her and was exalted with pride. There wasn't another mare to touch her, and all around he heard comments on her elegance, on her exquisite lines, on her gentle lovely face and the eager way that she ran.

"She's an all-out winner," a man near by said enthusiastically, and Paddy, with three weeks' wages staked, was unable to watch. His throat closed, he felt sick, and he had to turn away.

They were over the fifth fence and running to the sixth, and one of the leading horses was down and Vence had the glasses and at first couldn't see which and Paddy nearly died several deaths as he waited.

"Marazoa . . . not Zara," Vence said, and Paddy relaxed, but there were too many fences left and another horse was down and one of the jockeys was on the ground and the riderless mare was running on, running free, chasing the leaders, wanting to finish her race, likely to create havoc as she jumped alongside them, with no one to guide her path. She might bump them or crash into them. . . .

Paddy could no longer even pretend to look. He went to stand beside Honey, with his back to the race course and prayers racing through his head. Maybe it was wrong to pray for a horse to win a race, but arrah to goodness, honest to God, he would confess next Friday and the priest would absolve him and in any case, hadn't he himself put ten shillings on Zara for Father Anselm?

And Father Anselm was a great poker player too, and sometimes in the Bell, sitting there as at home as in his own house, he would play poker and sometimes nap, with Annie and Aaron and Adam, and hadn't Paddy heard him groan only the night before, "Holy Mary, lead me not into temptation," and then a moment later say, "I'll raise you a shilling." And surely if the priest himself put a shilling on a card game and some money on a horse, it couldn't be wicked to pray for Sam and Zara? Not for the horse to win perhaps, but for them to finish the race safely. . . .

Chris, standing beside Sue, was also breathless with excitement. Sam had to win, never mind Paddy's money. Chris didn't bet and wasn't starting, but he wanted the mare to do them credit and knew from his father how much the stud depended on her progeny. . . . Sue had grabbed Chris's hand in a vicious grip and was also unable to breathe, saying over and over, "Come on, Sam. Come on, Sam. Come on, Sam."

There were shouts from the crowd, and the mare flickered her ears uneasily, not sure that she liked the volume of noise, and Sam leaned to her ear and whispered to her, his voice soothing, and once more the two of them were alone and concentrating, aware of the free-running mare beside them, her saddle empty, but unbothered, and there was one horse in front, straining as they came to the last two fences and the straight finish, and another mare behind them was catching up and the third from last fence was upon them almost before Sam realized.

Up and over and on, but this time a fault that lost her ground as her foot slipped in the well-poached grass beyond the fence, and Sam gave her a hint of what he needed from her and she leaped forward in a smooth glide; her hooves spurned the grass beneath her and she and the mare that had come up behind were running neck and neck and there was one mare in front, and Sam thought that she might be tiring, as she had run in front for most of the way.

The second-to-last fence and his heart flying over and the mare following and he was back in the saddle and easing her again, asking her to run and she was running on strongly, as eager as at the start, annoyed by the frisking tail that flirted in front of her, challenging her as no animal had challenged her before. None could run so fast in Richard's stable.

The last fence. It was upon them and the mare met it right and flashed over and the horse beside her faltered and the riderless mare had vanished somewhere behind and another horse fell and Sam heard the cries that told him what had happened, but had no time to consider, no time for the fear that he might have fallen too, or that they might still come to grief in the last few hundred yards. He had to win.

There was another mare running beside them, her head level with Zara, and only a length in front was the leader. Sam was still lying close against the rail, which he had used as a guide to make sure the mare ran the shortest course, to help her to keep straight and to help himself too, so that he kept his advantage.

The thud of hooves was an insult. Sam settled down for the last long stretch, and his heels tapped the mare, asking her for her best. He was almost unseated. He had never dreamed there was such speed locked up inside her, and as she swept forwards, her acceleration was a physical shock, driving him too, so that he clung with his knees for dear life and then was seized with wild exultation, so that he thrust her along, glorying in the rush of air past his face, in the sudden surge of power, and aware of the mares behind her, now falling away, so that Zara was leading, Zara was hurtling towards the winning post, Zara was running first, Zara was running alone, no other beast able to stay beside her. There never had been such a mare. There never had been such a mare.

The words were echoed all round the race-track.

Vence, beside himself, kissed Honey's ears, and

Paddy threw his cap into the air and yodelled, and Sue clung to Chris, saying over and over, "They won. They won. They won."

They were running to greet him, and Sam was falling from the saddle and the mare was trembling and panting and wet with sweat and strangers were stroking her and Sue was kissing her, and she was immensely satisfied, having chased every other tail off the field and led in the end.

Richard, arriving late because his plane had been delayed by fog in London, had driven over with Jed and arrived to see his mare clear the last three fences and then speed to the finish as if powered by lightning, flashing swiftly past him with a glimpse of flying hooves and of Sam's set face. He came running across the racecourse to congratulate Sam and thump him until he almost felt sick.

"There never was such a mare."

Sam was in a dream. He turned to speak to Sue, and his eye was taken by a small knot of people just behind him, their faces dour. He glanced down. The mare that had followed them home lay stretched on the ground. She would never race again. It damped his excitement, and he touched Richard's arm, anxious to prevent him from voicing his own delight. Richard glanced across and stiffened.

"Burst her heart, quite literally," Jed said, coming over, his face grim. "She's been a good mare, too, and game to the end. She must have finished that race in agony."

Vence was rugging Zara, his own fervour killed.

"One of the jockeys has a broken leg," he said. "And they shot a mare at the first fence. She splintered a bone beyond repair."

"It's a tough game," Richard said. He patted Sam's

shoulder. "It was a well-run race. I think you'll find one or two people willing to give you a ride after that."

It was what Sam wanted. It was a dream come true, and yet, as he looked at the dead mare and her owner and jockey and trainer standing sorrowful beside her, he was conscious of curiously mixed sensations, and of the realization that triumph for one must always mean sorrow for another. Not everybody could win.

A moment later the owner and the trainer of the dead mare came to admire Zara and to congratulate them.

"She's beautiful," the other man said wistfully. He had lost more than money. He had been fond of his animal, and the jockey was tearful and unable to talk to anyone, and had gone away, silent, although he had gained second place, to complete the formalities, without his horse to share his honours.

"I'm not racing her again," Richard said. He could not take his eyes off the dead horse. "I want her for breeding. She's shown she has a turn of speed and that's all I want to know. She'll breed grand foals."

Paddy collected his money and came to join the others for the homeward journey, while Jed drove Richard back to the airport.

It was a curious return. They were simultaneously elated and depressed, unhappy at the waste of a good mare, who had shown her gallantry to the end. Sam was exhausted and slept all the way home, and Paddy, concentrating on his driving, his money warm in his pocket, summed up the day when they came into the yard and Nan and Jack Braithwaite and Adam ran to meet them.

"Arrah, we won," he said. "She's a turn of speed that would put a Rolls Royce to shame. But honest to God, it's a mug's game. The second mare died at the post, poor beast. Arrah, it's a hard world."

He and Vence took the mare and cosseted her, feeding her royally and removing the day's dust from her. She was very tired, standing with drooping head, and Sam, waking briefly, almost unable to move, stiff from the previous day's adventure, went to see her and see how she fared after her ordeal.

He stroked her and she bent her head to him. She had done her best for him, and she always would. Beside her, small and creamy-coated, Honey dreamed of buttercup meadows and summer sun, and of Velvet, in her own box close by.

That night, tired beyond belief, sunk in uneasy dreams, Sam rode the race again and finished it with the mare dropping beneath him, and it was Zara that lay on the ground, dead, and he could not rouse from the nightmare, and when he did his pillow was soaked in sweat, but he lay and shivered, and in the morning found his legs refused to take his weight.

The doctor, summoned hastily, examined him carefully.

"You've overworked your engine, lad," he said. "You need some rest . . . I should never have let you race yesterday."

Sam managed a wry grin.

"Nobody could have stopped me," he said.

His determination matched the mare's. Neither of them would ever give up while there was life and breath in their bodies. Lying in bed, he watched the sun come up the sky and lived the race again and knew that whatever happened and however he fared, he was born to race, even if racing killed him.

Richard, phoning from London to see how they all were, and giving the latest bulletin on Stella, told Vence that, as soon as she was ready, Zara could be taken to the stallion, and they would start her foal.

Vence went round the stable whistling. There was

nothing he wanted more. A foal to beat all foals, a foal to run faster than his mother had run, a foal that would win every race possible and gain the highest list of wins that had ever been known. A foal that would make the Proud stud famous throughout the world, and bring them honours and high prices, and ensure their future.

There would never be such a dam as Zara. He gave her a carrot and a dose of honey in her feed, and he stood and watched her eat, enthralled by her beauty, as proud as if she were his own.

CHAPTER *fifteen*

Life changed for everyone. Sam found a note from Jed asking him if he would care to ride his recently acquired five-year-old bay gelding, Major Fortune, in the races at Ascot at the beginning of March. Sam whistled as he worked, and borrowed Tarzan and rode across the hills to tell Mary Gregg of his good fortune.

Zara flirted with Midnight, and within a few weeks of her meeting with the stallion the laboratory report confirmed her pregnancy test, and Vence and Paddy treated her as if she were living gold, their hopes confirmed.

Richard had taken Stella to Bermuda, to recover from her operation in a climate that was warm and more bearable than the winter chills at home, and he read of their achievement in a letter and grinned happily.

"Good news?" Stella asked sleepily. She was often tired, and moved slowly, asking nothing more than to sit beside Richard and watch him. All her restlessness had vanished. She was quiet, a reflective image of her former self, needing constant reassurance. It was hard to get used to the change, but it was good to realize the bad days were over. She did not want to drink, and the people in the hotel found the couple cause for curious pondering, as she depended so much on Richard's presence and was desperately uneasy and unsure of herself if he was away. The general opinion was that they were a honeymoon couple, married late in life, until a retired colonel, talking to Richard at the bar one night, learned that they had a seventeen-year-old daughter. Sue's photograph dropped out of Richard's wallet.

"Why don't you and your wife join us after dinner?" he asked.

"My wife's recovering from a very difficult operation," Richard said. "She needs plenty of rest."

The mystery was solved, and people became more friendly, so that slowly Stella found her way back to the world again, having to relearn much that she had forgotten. The past was mercifully vague, a dim unpleasant memory that sometimes worried her but that Richard assured her was gone and did not matter. They had to find new ground for contact. They had forgotten how to communicate in the long years that had gone.

Richard glanced up when Stella asked if the news was good.

"Zara's definitely in foal," he said.

Stella looked thoughtfully at a sea so blue that it seemed unreal, and stretched herself, savouring the sun.

"Richard . . ." She did not want to ask, yet she felt that she must. "Would you call the foal Tempest, after the surgeon who operated on me? He's very interested in horses . . . he'd like to own one, one day. He told me about it when he came to see me. . . . We often talked about your horses. . . ."

"It's a very good idea," Richard said. He smiled down at her. She was curiously defenceless and vulnerable, much more easily hurt and unable to defend herself. Tempest had said she would lack both drive and initiative and they would have to do her thinking and planning for her.

"Perhaps he could have a share in the foal . . ." Stella said.

"The foal isn't born yet. Not for nearly a year . . . Let's wait and see what happens." Richard hated to plan ahead. Too many snags were possible.

Later that day they met the colonel and his wife, the colonel full of enthusiasm because he had bought a stick from a native shop. He showed it to Richard. The stick had a carved head, a man's head, ugly and leering, and in one sickening minute Richard remembered his own snake stick and his absurd and growing conviction that it was unlucky. The stick was in the shed at home, where he had hidden it among the rubbish. It was still there, with the power to wreck his plans.

His parents' deaths, his grandfather's accident, and Stella's fall all seemed to add together to disaster, to a curse on the family, a curse that could be embodied in a carved and evil hickory stick. He wished he were home. He would burn the thing as soon as he got there. Meanwhile, they had still to fly back, and Sue was there, with the thing close to her and the power in it that, in this atmosphere of unreality, he had begun to fear. He wished that Sue were telepathic. If he sent a wire to tell her to burn the stick she would think him mad. Or would she?

It was Sarah who remembered the stick. She had been watching Zara grazing in the field, and Vence had come up to her and stood beside her.

"Letter from the boss," he said. "His wife's doing well and they'll be home next Monday. Sue'll be pleased. She's missed her dad. Nice to think bad luck's ended."

Sue and Chris had gone out onto the hills with
Storm. Sarah thought of them, and of the luck of the
Prouds, and remembered the stick. Where had she
seen it? She was going to find the thing and burn it,
no matter what they thought of it, antique and valuable
or not. It was unlucky. It had been made by wicked
hands and cursed and brought evil to the family.

Maybe they'd never even miss it. If they asked she
would tell them. If not . . . she would not bother to
confess. She was doing it for their own good. Nasty old
thing. She hardly cared to touch it. She turned and
went determinedly to hunt for it. Time the luck
changed, and it never would with that around.

"Where are you going?" Jim asked, meeting her some
minutes later in the tack room. It was not there, and
she was not going to rest till she'd found it. Surely it
hadn't gone off to Bermuda?

"Nowhere," Sarah said. No use telling Jim. He'd
laugh at her, though he had his own superstitions, and
would never start a new venture on a Friday or put the
number thirteen on a loose box. He had insisted that
the loose boxes were lettered and not numbered. That
way, there never was a thirteen.

She passed Tarzan's box and looked briefly at the
neat typed history telling his age and the details of his
breeding and noting that his diet had changed during
the present week, as he had shown signs of colic.

"Only need an epidemic to put us right back where
we started," Sarah thought and went on hunting, more
determined than ever to find the source of their troubles and put an end to them forever.

Out on the hill, Chris and Sue released Storm and
watched him fly overhead, while Brutus played the fool,
hunting for rabbits with as little knowledge of the right
way to do it as any untrained pup. He sniffed at one

hole and tried to excavate another, and chased a bird,
and then lay and panted, exhausted by his efforts.

Storm always returned to the lure. He had no more
desire for freedom, and Sue and Chris exercised him
daily, flying him above them and swinging the rook
wings time and time again, flicking it away from him at
the last minute, ensuring that he swooped and circled
and kept himself fit. He had just flown up for the third
time when Brutus started a hare from her form in the
heather.

The dog was as unnerved as the hare, and as she ran
zigzag he stood stock-still, staring, and then gave hopeless chase. Storm, above him, saw the running hare and
left the lure and chased her, his shadow on the grass
driving her to momentary panic and then to clearer
thinking as memory stood her well, and she leaped sideways and doubled on her tracks and then ran in circles,
increasing the diameter, leaping over the ground, and
as the bird's shadow fell on her, twisting and backtrack-
ing until Brutus, hunting by scent, was confounded and
gave up, and the bird, becoming tired, stooped and
missed, and the hare with one final leap went to ground
in a hole under the wall and watched, her ears pricked
forward to catch the suggestion of a sound, her eyes
staring, her body panting.

Storm came back to the lure. He was hungry, and
this was no way to get fed. Sue removed him from the
feathered bait to a piece of meat held in her hand and
then sat beside Chris, who was lying against the wall,
which trapped the faint spring sunshine, hinting of a future summer. There were celandines starring the grass,
out of the wind.

"I'll be glad when Mother and Dad are safely home,"
Sue said, watching the bird tear at the meat, which he
held steady on her glove with his thick talons. He stood

to swallow and looked at her thoughtfully, the shreds of steak dangling from his beak. His amber eyes considered her, his head on one side, and then he bent again to feed.

"They'll be okay," Chris said lazily, contemplating a minute insect that was making its devious way up the stone wall. He watched Sue contentedly.

"I'm going back to school," he said, a moment later.

Sue rubbed a finger between the bird's wings. He was no longer keen for his food but was eating contemplatively, slowly, losing interest.

"Why?" she asked.

"I'm going to be a vet. That needs A levels, so I'll have to work pretty hard. And when I'm qualified we'll breed horses. You can do that, and I'll have my practice. It'll be fun."

Sue looked at him thoughtfully.

"Are you proposing or something?" she said finally.

Chris's face was astonished.

"No," he said at last. "I'm telling you. Don't you think it's a good idea? It'll be years before we can get married. . . . I've got another year to do at school and then five years in vet college. So you'll have lots of time to learn all about breeding horses and donkeys. You might even persuade your father to let you have a horse or two of your own to start us off."

Sue found her lips were twitching. She had often dreamed of a proposal of marriage, but had never visualized one like this. She knew she would wait for Chris and knew too that he had had no need to ask her. The understanding that had sprung between them was too deep for words. She bent towards him and smoothed his mouth with her finger, and he put up his face and kissed her lips.

Storm bit his ear.

Sarah had found the stick. It was in the shed, pushed behind the rubbish, and while she was at it, it was almost spring, and time for cleaning, and the shed could do with a turnout, and if she burnt all the rubbish that needed burning no one was going to notice the old stick. She looked at the evil little man's head and the twining snake head, and pulled it out from behind the mess of planks and an old clothesbasket and two trugs and a hoe with a broken handle. The whole lot could go.

She took the things one by one into the yard and stacked them on the wheelbarrow. She felt guilty, knowing that Richard Proud had prized the stick and that it had been considered a family heirloom, but she was not going to let a feeling of guilt stop her.

She had a patch in the garden that she always used for bonfires. There were some garden clippings on it now that could start the blaze. She piled the rubbish high, the stick in the middle of it, and set fire to the lot.

She was leaving nothing to chance. She took a stout pole and poked at the flames, and deep in the heart of them saw the little head and the shining eyes from the man and the snake. Pictures glowed about them so that snake head and man head were part of a hellfire that shimmered and flickered and burnt, and quite suddenly there was a fusillade of shots and Sarah leaped backwards away from the fire, pain searing her arm, blood pouring from torn flesh.

She stared about her, terrified, and Jim and Paddy came running. Jim grabbed her.

"Sarah. What the devil was that?"

"The devil himself, I'm thinking," Sarah said. She felt sick and the pain was almost unbearable. Jim and Paddy each put an arm round her as she stood swaying.

Paddy glanced at the bonfire and saw the last dying flash from the snake stick. The two heads were interwoven, the twin pairs of wicked eyes glittered inimically, and then with a sigh and a rush they fell into ashes.

"You burned the stick," Paddy said.

"Aye. It was evil and I wanted to change the luck of the Prouds," Sarah answered. She was glad she had done it, but could not understand what had happened to her.

"Woman!" Jim shouted. He almost choked. "The stick was full of cartridges. It's where the old man kept his spare ammunition. We couldn't unscrew the head and get them out so we left them there. You've been shot! What in the world did you burn it for?"

Even at the last the stick had triumphed.

"How was I to know?" Sarah asked.

And fainted.

CHAPTER *sixteen*

Richard was thankful that the stick had been burned, and horrified to learn what had happened to Sarah. She was philosophical.

"Always said it were evil," she said. "And now I proved it."

During the year that followed Richard began to think she had been right. The four colts put in for the Newmarket sales fetched the highest prices he had ever received; Sam rode for Jed and his friends and rode three winners out of eight mounts and began to ride for other trainers. He was now apprenticed and learning fast. Nobody could deny he had quality.

Chris went back to school determined to do well enough to gain his university place, and by the time he had started in Liverpool, at the veterinary school, Zara was a plump and placid matron and the routine of the stud revolved round her needs. The foal was going to be the best in the country, the best in Europe, the best in the world.

Alan Tempest, calling in to visit them on his way to see his mother, found Stella in the stables with Vence, helping to prepare the mare's feed. She had regained her old love of horses and learned once more to handle them, although she refused to ride, much too afraid that she might fall again and injure her head. It was enough to be part of their world, to help Vence and Paddy and try to make up to Richard for the dimly remembered bitter years that she knew must still be vivid to him, although for her they were mercifully blurred.

She could not understand how she could have changed so much. The decorations of the house appalled her, and she and Sue went through her clothes.

"I can't have worn this," she said in horror, staring at one particularly daring and brilliantly coloured dress. "It doesn't even suit me."

Sue, aware that her mother needed immense reassurance and shaken by the change in her, had nodded her head. Stella laughed.

"I don't believe it," she said. "We'd better go through everything and throw out the most awful."

"Buy some more," Richard suggested, coming into the room to see them staring at the heaped clothing on the bed. "I'll take you both out for the day and you can both buy yourselves one or two outfits."

It had been one of the happiest days that Sue had spent, and, on the way home, Stella asked Richard wistfully if he would mind very much if Paddy and Vence painted every wall in the house in light colours to hide the startling colour schemes. Soon they were all wielding paint brushes, and Sue's room became a restful haven with white walls that helped mute the colours of the bright carpet. Richard brought her a large rug that hid most of it, and the bed hid the rest. Sarah dyed the spread to blend, and the modern chairs were put in the flat over the stable, which Richard was preparing for a new man who was to help in the stud. Adam was staying but had become increasingly feeble. He could never be severed from animals, but to keep him working was

out of the question. He now had one big room at the
end, beyond the flat.

The house became once more a place in which to relax. Stella's obsessional tidiness vanished, and when Pru had kittens agreed at once that Sue should have the little tom, once he had been house trained and provided he was neutered. By the time Tempest visited them, Tuppence was part of their lives and sat in the stables at Stella's feet, watching the world he had inherited with bright amused eyes, occasionally commenting loudly in his Siamese voice about one or another of the many strange objects that caught his attention. Zara and Honey both watched him with as much interest as he had for them, and Honey, in particular, occasionally answered, his hoarse bray startling the kitten, who promptly ran and hid behind a box and could only be enticed out by a piece of string dangled to distract him.

There was little time for worry. Stella was involved and amused and content at last, and Tempest, watching her, was very glad that he had been snowbound by some miraculous coincidence and able to help her regain her sanity.

"Zara looks very well," he said, stroking the mare's warm neck. He grinned. "I envy you. There's nothing in the world like a stable and horses of your own."

"We're calling her foal Tempest," Stella said. "Proud Tempest . . . don't you think it sounds good?"

Alan Tempest looked at her, unable to find words. It was a sudden heartwarming thought that she was repaying him. It was not often that he could follow up a case and find out what had happened as the result of his work.

"We thought you might like a share in the foal," Richard said. "It'll be some time before he shows a profit, but we think he will. . . . Midnight has run plenty of races in his time and won a good many. He was unlucky enough to be in the same year as two of the greatest horses of all time and not quite able to catch them . . . but he did marvellously well. And Zara could have run every other horse in the business today off the race-courses if we'd let her. . . . I'm sure of that."

"I can't wait for the foal to arrive," Tempest said. "When's it due?"

"At the end of February. We'll send you a telegram when it's born." Richard led the way into the house. A warm fire glowed in the hearth. It was chill even for November. Winter had come soon, and summer was only a memory. Sarah brought tea and scones and tea cakes and joked about her gunshot scar, and went away again.

"It's a funny thing," Richard said. "Just before she burned the stick I was wishing I could send Sue a telegram and ask her to get rid of it. . . . I had a thing about that stick and so had Sarah. We both thought it was evil and brought bad luck."

" 'There are more things in Heaven and Earth, Horatio, than are dreamt of in your philosophy,' " Tempest quoted. "I for one would never question that."

He thought of his words again as he drove down the lonely road that bisected the moor, and an owl slipped out of the night and flew beside his car, keeping him company, and dropped away to stoop into the ditch and vanish to eat its kill. It was difficult not to believe that some things were foreordained and that others were caused by unknown influences.

He thought of the foal and looked forward to the spring and to discovering the little creature that had been bred from Zara and from Midnight, and Milton's words suddenly crossed his mind. He could rarely resist a quotation: "From Cerberus and blackest Midnight

born . . ."—he trusted the foal would not be melan-
choly. He laughed and accelerated, and the darkness
sped away from him, chased by his headlights.

Christmas that year was a time for rejoicing. Stella
was well enough to enjoy the celebrations, to choose
her own presents for everyone and make her own sur-
prises, and she gave a small dinner party on New Year's
Eve for the Howarths and the Hanbulls and for Chris.

Chris and Sue spent most of the time with their
heads together, making plans and talking eagerly, and
Richard caught his wife's eye and then exchanged
glances with the two Hanbulls. The same thought
crossed all their minds, and they hoped that their sus-
picions were correct. It would be ideal for everyone.

The two vanished before midnight, and came in as
the clock struck twelve.

"We want to get engaged," Chris said. He looked at
them defiantly. "We won't get married till I'm qualified
. . . only . . . we'd like to make it official. A pledge."

Richard went to find champagne, and, as he brought
the bottle in, Chris's expression eased, and he caught his
mother's eye and then his father's and looked across at
Stella.

"You all look smug," he said accusingly, and Jed
grinned delightedly.

"They feel smug," he said and lifted his glass.

It had been a good Christmas. The days afterwards
sped by, busy with the stud, as mares came to visit Midnight and the foals were born, but all the thoughts and
hopes of everyone in the stable centred round Zara.

She was exercised gently, walked round the yard to
keep her fit and to keep her supple. She was fed like a
queen, her diet carefully balanced and all kinds of titbits added to ensure that her appetite remained keen.
She was plump and sleek and thriving, and Paddy bet

Vence a pound to a shilling that the foal would be male.

Snow fell again and blocked the roads, and one night, late in February, Richard woke to hear knocking on the door. Paddy stood there, covered in snow and shivering. He had stayed on to take his turn at watching the mares. Someone always sat up at night to ensure that none foaled alone. They were valuable assets.

"I think Zara's started," he said. It had been obvious for most of the day that the foal was ready to be born. It had slipped into the birth position and the mare had been restless and uncomfortable, unable to understand what was happening to her, pawing the straw uneasily, not wanting even Honey near her.

Richard had moved her into the foaling room, and Paddy kept watch.

"She's not alone?" Richard said.

Paddy shook his head.

"Jim came over. He's with her now. It's not near yet, I'm sure, but it will be born tonight."

It was bitterly cold. The wind raging across the moors blew the snow into their faces, and they plunged calf-deep into newly fallen layers that covered the old. The stable was only a short walk from the house, but it seemed miles, and the wicked chill knocked the breath from them. The warmth was unnerving as they came through the door into the little room where Vence was watching.

"She might be better for company," Jim said, looking through the glass at the mare, who was lying in the straw, her head thrusting uneasily, her eyes anxious. "She needs comforting."

He went through to her, and she watched him as he knelt beside her, his hands soothing, feeling along her straining body. The foal was alive and fighting to escape, and the mare's muscles were striving violently to expel it. Her rolling eyes told of the fright that was mastering her, the fear of unknown forces taking her over against her will, the impossibility of understanding what was happening to her or of knowing that within hours she would once more be free from pain with her own foal beside her. It was something she would have to learn, and there was some time to go.

The wind, howling round the buildings, whipping up the snow, drove against roof and window, and the stable fittings rattled and shook. The scream and whine as the gale fled round the stables alarmed the mare further, and Richard knelt beside her too and stroked her neck and talked to her gently. He had seen many foals born, but the sight never ceased to have poignancy. Thoroughbred mares were sensitive, and there was always pain. They stared with uncomprehending eyes, and sweat darkened the soft hide, and there was nothing that could be done to ease the moment or speed the birth.

"Hope there's no complication," Vence said uneasily. "The road's blocked and the vet could never get here. They'll need the snow-plough in the morning before he can come. And I want him to look at her tomorrow."

The pride of their stables, their hope, their future, now torn by torment and without any possibility of aid. Worry knifed at Richard. Ill luck from an old stick? What tomfool idiocy. Luck came and luck went and there was no knowing how or why. There might be worse round the corner. The foal might die, although at the moment he could hear its heartbeat, loud, insistent, and steady when he listened. If that heartbeat failed . . .

He went to the door and looked out into the darkness, and nothing was to be seen but velvet black and swirling flakes drifting out of an uncaring sky. No chance of help. There were others worse off. Others marooned, women in labour too, cut off by the night. The papers would be full of their plight in the morning, and his was only a small matter, beside theirs. But not for them. Nor for the mare, struggling to her feet, wild-eyed, head tossing, pawing again and again at the straw, trying to rid herself of the violence that racked her.

Richard began to recite aloud, words from old poems coming to his mind, anything to soothe her, to take away a little of the misery, to give her reassurance, to remind her of his presence. Paddy had gone upstairs to catch up with his sleep, and was catnapping uneasily on a camp bed in one of the rooms above the stable, more than half awake, listening for noises from downstairs, as racked by worry as Richard and Jim Vence, as anxious for Zara's safety, for her future, his future, tied up with the Proud stud. Sometimes his wife wondered if she had a husband. His job, his time spent with the horses, was a dedication, and in emergency he was always on call, ready to soothe or to stay with an ailing beast, just as Jim or Richard would stay.

Adam was resting in the room beyond his old flat. That was ready for the new man who would start in a few weeks' time, after returning from a tour abroad with three racing mares who had been taken to an Italian stud. He was tired of constant travelling, as he worked for a firm that dealt mainly in exporting horses, and he wanted a more settled job. Adam did not mind, so long as they did not put him into a home for old men, away from beasts. He could never live in a cage. He heard the pawing mare and dressed and went downstairs, unable to sleep, unable to take his mind off her.

He made coffee for the two men.

" 'Tis a dree business," he said, bringing them their drink and looking at the mare, who tossed her head uneasily.

"Sarah made some sandwiches," Jim said. He went to find the packet and shared it out, but Richard could not eat. The mare was struggling harder, and he was afraid for her. She was so delicately made, and he was afraid the foal might be too big to be born, or might tear her, and they had no chance of qualified help. As far as he could feel there was no sign of trouble in its presentation . . . everything appeared to be the right way round.

He was tired, but there was no time for sleep. The hours to dawn stretched endless, and there was nothing in the world but the frightened mare and the whip and whine and whistle of the demented wind, and the soft flutter-fall of sliding snow from the steep roof.

"Get some sleep, Jim," he said at last. "I'll call you."

"Ah'll wait oop," Adam said. "No need for sleep when tha's so old."

He sat at the desk, his thoughts roaming back over the years, remembering wistfully that once he had been young, that then horses had been the only transport, the most important creatures in the world. So many horses on the streets, pulling the cabs and coaches, and every man owned some kind of nag unless he was too poor to count in the scheme of life.

All those years ago, trudging to school only when the weather was wet, leaving to work with his father when he was ten, being apprenticed to old man Proud, and a right old devil he'd been though bettermer some he could mention. Funny, looking back to the days when only Parson in the village had been able to read, and on Sundays before church they congregated in the pub and Parson read the news . . . news of strange laws and reforms and factory acts, and news of wars, meaningless wars that he'd never found the rights and wrongs about, though he had fought in two of them. Too old for anything now. Too old even to sit with the mare and help her find ease. Just waiting to go, like all his cronies, gone long ago, and only he left, with no one to share his memories, just a doddering old man in a chimney corner, his legs refusing to obey him, his head mumbly with thoughts that drifted in unbidden and drifted out again.

Like yesterday it was, the day they brought old Mr. Proud home from hunting, lying on a stretcher. A fine clear frosty October day and the scent lying strong on the ground and the fox flying from the hounds and the hounds running free, their music belling over the fields. Been a bad day that. Adam dozed, and the fire threw reflections on the wall, and in the stable Richard agonized with the mare and longed to free her from pain, but there was nothing he could do, nothing to ease her, nothing to bring the foal more quickly, nothing to help.

He wanted to smoke, but he dared not leave her. She was quieter now, and he dried the sweat from her with a big rough towel that he had brought with him. It was better than using wisped straw.

There was a movement behind him. He thought that Paddy or Jim had come back, and did not turn his head. He was startled when Stella came towards the mare, dressed in warm slacks and a thick jersey.

"I couldn't sleep," she said. "Richard . . . can't you do anything?"

"I wish I could." Richard looked grim. He hated the ordeal that the beasts endured. It was never easy, and he never became used to watching them suffer. He stroked the smooth neck again and murmured to her, and she relaxed briefly.

"I didn't know it was like this . . . it's as bad as for women. . . ."

Richard said nothing. He remembered Sue's birth vividly, remembered wishing he had known nothing of the trials of motherhood, but he had supervised the birth pangs of too many mares.

"She'll have forgotten everything within an hour of the birth," Stella said. "I thought I'd never forget while Sue was coming, but afterwards, it was hard to remember anything except that she was there . . . and life was wonderful. Do you remember?"

Richard nodded. The mare was listening to them, her ears flickering forwards when they spoke.

"Can the vet get here?" Stella asked.

Richard shook his head.

"Just have to pray," he said. "Sometimes I wonder if the horses are worth it . . . so much time, and so much money, and so many easier ways of earning a living."

"But none you'd like," Stella said. "I can't imagine you in an office . . . or a factory. Or anywhere but with horses."

She sat on the edge of the manger.

"Will it be long?"

"I don't know . . . why don't you go back to bed?"

"I can't sleep," Stella said. "I lay there, remembering, and things began to come back to me, things I'd forgotten . . . before I had that operation. I don't want to remember. I can't believe they happened to me. . . ."

"They don't matter," Richard said. "We've all forgotten. Everyone has. It's now that's important . . . never what's past."

"Richard!"

The mare was on her feet, her eyes momentarily panic-wild. A titanic convulsion seized her and Richard went to her head and spoke to her, but she was beyond reason as wave upon wave of blinding pain sent her beyond the reach of his help, beyond all knowledge of the world about her.

Stella was staring at her, sure that she would damage herself, that she would rupture some vital organ, certain that no living body could stand such strain.

Her tail lifted. The foal appeared, and within a few seconds, as her muscles contorted so viciously that their effort was apparent, it was part way out, and Richard moved to help it and guide it gently to the straw so that it lay beside her, slimed and wrapped in the membrane that covered it during birth.

"Fetch Paddy and Jim," Richard said. He had no time for Stella or for anyone else, and he bent to free the foal's head and clear its mouth and nostrils and make sure it was breathing and then went back to the trembling mare, as she stood, slack and exhausted, head down, panting with her efforts.

"The foal's born."

Adam was there and Paddy was there and Jim was bringing warm water to sponge Zara, and Paddy was welcoming the foal and cleaning it, watching with amazed disbelief as the small head moved wearily, the tiny ears flickered, the first deep breaths shook the little body. He wanted to sing, to shout, to yell his exultation. This was achievement. Satisfaction. Deep content.

There was no time to rejoice. The mare was lying in the straw and she needed cleaning, and the foal needed attention, and Paddy began to rub him down with straw. Vence brought the salt and sprinkled the baby. The mare would lick the salt eagerly and then continue to lick the foal and establish her relationship with him.

She had lifted her head, and was watching Paddy, her eyes puzzled. The foal's ears were moving, and quite suddenly he lifted his head and made a tiny, curiously infantile sound. Zara pricked her ears.

She was distracted by Stella, who, on Vence's instruc-

tions, had made an oatmeal gruel well laced with salt,
and held it for her to drink. She was ravenous after her
efforts and took the food eagerly. Richard relaxed. She
was unharmed by her experience, and showed none of
the symptoms of shock that he had feared. Paddy was
watching the foal, who, now clean and dry and breathing easily, was looking curiously about him at this
strange world into which he had arrived so suddenly
and so violently.

He moved his legs. Slowly he flexed each one in turn,
and then his small body struggled to stand. But standing was too difficult, he had had a hard time and he
was tired, and with a deep sigh he flopped on the straw
again and stretched out his head.

Vence had brought warm packs to soothe the mare.
She was easier now and comforted, and aware of the
people round her. There were too many of them and
they must leave her in peace, but she seemed unbothered. Stella went outside to watch through the window,
and once he was sure that the foal was clean and dry
Paddy joined her, and they were both fascinated as the
foal began once more to struggle to his feet, this time
rising half way from the straw before deciding that he
needed more time.

Zara saw him properly and her head turned and she
stared at him and then stared at Richard, her eyes brilliant with intelligence, so that he could have sworn she
was asking what this creature might be that had suddenly come to her in the night. She stood, and moved
across the straw, and looked down at the foal. He gazed
up at her, blue eyes astonished, as she towered above
him.

This was the critical moment. She might reject him.
She might accept him. She might be doubtful, not sure
what to do, and Richard held his breath.

The foal lifted his head. He was even more exquisite

than they had hoped, his coat darker than his mother's, his body beautifully formed and delicate, every line perfect.

Quite unexpectedly, he yawned, and the mare stepped backwards, totally astounded. She moved forwards again and this time her nose brushed his, and her tongue, questing, licked the top of his soft head, and the expression in her eyes changed so suddenly that Richard, watching her, was unable to rationalize what had happened. She was aware of the foal, and her licking tongue did not need the salt to tell her to claim her own. The softness in the dark eyes was enough to tell Richard that. She was exalted, and she looked at Richard as if asking for praise, and he stroked her and petted her and called her small endearing little names that she knew and seemed to like, and, as the foal once more struggled to reach his feet, she gazed at him, delighted, knowing he was her own, that this was the result of the long hours of pain and that she was rapturous in her new motherhood.

They left the pair alone, and Richard brought out the whisky and gave everyone a small tot. It had been a long vigil. Stella had vanished, and he thought she had gone back to bed, but she had gone running to the house, shaking Sue awake.

"Zara's had her foal . . ." she said, and excitement was paramount, and Sue jumped from bed and flung on trousers and jersey and the two of them ran back through the snow, not heeding the wind that whined and blustered or the driving blizzard, coming in out of the chill into the warmth of the stables to look through the window, while Sue stared at the newcomer, unable to take her eyes off him.

"He's heaven," she said.

"Honest to God, that's what the mare thinks," Paddy

said. He was elated. It might have been his foal. They had never had such a foal . . . so exquisite, so perfect, so obviously an aristocrat.

An hour later, Tempest stood on his feet and tried to move, but his legs betrayed him and he looked comically dismayed. Everyone had gone back to bed but Richard, and he watched through the door and then went inside, wondering if Zara might resent him, might show her newly acquired mother pride by a hefty kick, but she greeted him as always with a tiny nibble of her lips, and he rewarded her with sugar and went to the tottering foal and helped him stand, and watched him reach for milk.

Milk was not forthcoming, for he had found his mother's knee, and Richard put out a hand to guide him and found his finger taken into the small mouth and sucked fiercely. He laughed, and showed the foal where his first meal could be found, and went away again, watching through the window to ensure that all was well. The mare could not take her eyes away from her son.

She watched every movement, watched him drink, and then watched him settle on the straw again, already weary. The afterbirth had come away cleanly and there was fresh straw on the ground, and Richard was tired. It had been a long night. He sat by the window. There might still be trouble, a chance of haemorrhage or of difficulty with the foal, but he was thankful when Paddy came to relieve him and he took his turn on the camp bed upstairs.

In the morning sun shone on the snow and the mare was lying beside the foal, with the tiny creature tucked close against her body. She could not look away lest it vanish. She was aware of every movement, of the gentle breathing, of its head turning when it woke, of its listening ears, of its faintest sound. There was no trouble with suckling, no trouble with either of them, and soon the spring would chase away the snow and she could teach her foal to run, to race, to strengthen his muscles, to learn his business, to become the fastest and fleetest colt in the country. He was glorious.

He was glorious. Everyone had peeped through the observation window. Sam had managed to make his way through the drifts and was already daydreaming of the time to come when he would ride Proud Tempest to the cheers of enormous crowds and his name would head the jockey lists and the foal would top the winning horses.

Sarah had come to admire him, and the vet had followed the snow-plough and was as delighted as the mare with her progeny.

Far away in London a message relayed by his mother was telegraphed through to Alan Tempest at the hospital where he was operating, and Matron, taking it down, was shocked. Tempest was a bachelor.

"Congratulations. It's a boy. Proud," the telegram said, and although she looked at him for an explanation he thrust the message in his pocket, grinning, and did not explain.

That night, going home, he thought with satisfaction of the mare in her Yorkshire home and the foal that was partly his beside her. Proud Tempest. No man could ask for better reward.

The mare, not knowing anything of their hopes and fears, bent her head to her son, and he lifted his to her, and then, suddenly aware that legs were meant for running, astonished her by a small leap and quick frisk in the air, and a second later, he was sucking ferociously, his small tail weaving frantically in the air as he savoured the warm milk.

Zara blew at him, and Richard, looking in at them,
sighed deeply.

There never had been such a mare.

There never had been such a foal.

Zara gazed up at him, her brown eyes glowing.

She was as well aware as he that this was a foal to treasure, a foal to give pride to everyone who saw him, a foal beyond price.

Tempest curled in the straw, quite unconscious of the hopes of all the stud that were focused on his small and exquisite body. His ears moved in dreams, and the mare dropped beside him, and rested her head against him, and drowsed in the thin rays of the early spring sun that angled through the stable window, burnishing chestnut coat to gold and sleeking the bay of the foal's darker colouring, and they slept, knowing the promise of warm days to come.